CHAMPAGNE KISSES

KRISTA LAKES

ZIRCONIA PUBLISHING, INC.

ABOUT THIS BOOK

In the summer of 1990, Rachel Weber spent a week down on the Florida coast, soaking up the sun's rays while she waited for her life to begin. It was there that she met Dean Sherman, a handsome, muscular soldier with crystal blue eyes. The two spent a week together full of champagne kisses that only ended when Operation Desert Storm forced Dean to choose between his duty and his love. He chose duty.

Twenty years later, Rachel figured it was just summer love, but she never forgot those eyes. As personal assistant to powerful billionaire Jack Saunders, she never expected Dean to walk into her office after being hired as Jack's personal bodyguard. Even though she had spent the last two decades trying to forget Dean, she found herself falling for him once again.

When fate forced both Rachel and Dean to choose yet again between love and duty, Rachel had to decide between the man she had always loved and the family that had become her life. She knew she couldn't have both, but she knew she wouldn't be happy with just one. Would she choose love, or be forever haunted by the memory of those Champagne Kisses?

This thrilling romance novel brings the cast of the best-selling novels Saltwater Kisses, Rainwater Kisses, and Freshwater Kisses back for an epic and timeless love story.

∾

I was shocked. "You're going to war? Why didn't you tell me?" I asked.

"Because this is a vacation. Because I didn't want to think about it. Because I thought that you wouldn't want to hang out with me if you thought of me as a trained killer instead of as a pretty face." He smiled, but it was an empty smile.

I laughed. "Don't be ridiculous. I never thought of you as a pretty face," I said. I started to laugh at my own joke, but I couldn't. Instead, I began to bawl openly, leaning into his shoulder. I didn't want him to go anywhere, and I certainly didn't want him to go to war.

Dean let me cry, stroking my hair gently. The fire began to go out in front of us, having consumed all the fuel that had been put into it. My heart felt the same way. In one week, I had known such intense highs that my heart had burned like a star, and now that it was starved of fuel, I felt it being extinguished.

I moved my head from Dean's shoulder. He tried to hide it as he wiped a tear away, but I knew. I looked at him. The dying light of the fire was just enough for me to see those crystal clear blue eyes. "Make love to me, Dean. Make love to me like this is the last night we'll ever spend together..."

∾

Also don't miss "Wishful Kisses", a novella based on Kim and Tony, at the end of this book!

Don't forget to sign up for <u>my newsletter</u>! You'll be the first to see my new covers, comment on new books of mine, and always know when books are available for free or on sale!

CHAMPAGNE KISSES

CHAPTER 1

 resent Day

THE CURSOR BLINKED STEADILY on the laptop screen in front of me, but I barely saw the dark pixels repeatedly dimming against the stark whiteness. I couldn't focus on writing the memo Jack requested, or even the website I had up in the background. My thoughts weren't even organized or even actual thoughts; I was just letting nothingness sit in my brain. The blank thoughts were a pleasant respite from the emotions running through the house.

A hand settling on my shoulder roused me from my silent thoughts. Jack Saunders, my boss and friend, gave me a small smile.

"How's that memo coming, Rachel?" he asked.

I sighed. "It's not. What did the doctor say?"

Jack's face fell a little. He sat down at the kitchen table next to me and played with the edge of the big wooden table. I could have worked anywhere in the Saunders' mansion, but I preferred the kitchen's warmth and sunny feeling in the mornings. The big country-style table was comfortable and I could hear the sounds of the house without being disturbed. Big bay windows let in the morning sun, the leaves outside were just starting to turn orange and rust. I loved being in upstate New York in the fall.

"It's not looking good. He says it's probably only a matter of days at this point." His voice stayed even, but the sharp lines of his tightened jaw betrayed his anguish. I reached over and put my hand on top of his, sharing his pain. His hazel eyes stared out the window, but I knew he wasn't looking at the trees. Jack and his father had played football under those trees. I could almost see them now, the older Saunders man chasing his eldest son around, the two of them laughing in the orange light.

"Does Robbie know?" In my mind's eye, the younger brother joined Jack and his father. The two boys tackled the bigger man and all three of them rolled around in the leaves as their laughter echoed through the years. Although I was Jack's senior by sixteen years, they had occasionally let me join them. Jack and Robbie ran the ball against Daniel and I. Somehow, the boys always managed to win.

"He knows it's bad," Jack said. "I tried to call him, but he won't answer and he ditched his security again. Probably out on his boat." Jack tried to keep the anger out of his voice. Even though the two brothers looked similar, tall with sandy brown hair and strong features, they couldn't be more different. Jack's devotion to the company his father had started was in sharp contract to Robbie, who wanted nothing to do with being responsible for anything more than his boat.

"Don't be mad at him, Jack," I said. "This is hard for him, too," I said.

Jack mumbled something about Robbie really needing to grow up. I sighed. This was a common source of tension between the two brothers. Jack had been groomed for responsibility from the day he was born, whereas Robbie had been mostly left to his own devices. I always got the feeling that Mr. and Mrs. Saunders just never knew what to do with Robbie. Now the owner and CEO of DS Oil and Gas, Jack ran it with a sure hand, while the tabloids portrayed Robbie as a drunken playboy who spent all his time sailing. I knew the two brothers loved one another, but their different priorities made it difficult for them to agree on anything.

"Jack?" Emma's voice called from down the hallway. Jack straightened in his seat and turned as his beautiful wife entered the kitchen. "Jack, you left your phone in the study. It rang, so I answered for you. You're needed at the office."

Jack's shoulders sagged. I knew the last place he wanted to be was at the office, but the company was his responsibility. Emma came behind him and wrapped her arms around his shoulders, gently kissing his cheek. Her long, dark hair spilled across his shoulder as she loved on him. His lip twitched into a small smile after she whispered something in his ear. I honestly enjoyed watching them; I had witnessed their courtship from the day Jack had brought her to New York after meeting her on vacation.

Emma and Jack had met on a tropical beach vacation a little over a year and a half before. Unknown to everyone in the Saunders' family, they had decided to get married on a beach just for fun. It was out of character for my usually pragmatic and responsible Jack, but he kept telling me it was an act of rebellion that wasn't supposed to have consequences. Since it wasn't a legal ceremony, it would have ended there, except the tabloids were given pictures. I had been up to my eyeballs trying to keep that from exploding into a PR nightmare.

I hadn't been sure of Emma's motives when I flew out to Iowa to pick her up and bring her to New York for damage control, but she turned out to be genuinely warm and full of integrity. It was easy to love Emma. She was undemanding, and fell in love with Jack for *Jack*. She loved him for him, and not for his money. I couldn't have asked for someone better to be with the man I considered a little brother. I had cried tears of joy at their wedding, knowing their love story was one for the ages.

"Do you need me to go with you?" I asked, mentally prepping the things I would need to get together for a trip into the city. I was Jack's personal assistant. His right hand man, so to speak. If he needed something done, I was the one he turned to. I had been looking after his interests since he was a boy.

He shook his head. "No, we've been waiting on the new contracts from Dubai to come in. I just need to sign them and make sure they are correct. I would rather have you here, with Dad. If anything happens..."

"Then Rachel and I will take care of things," Emma said. She kissed the top of his head, and he seemed to draw strength from her.

"I'll make sure Raoul keeps the helicopter on standby for you," I said, pulling out my phone and typing messages that would alert his helicopter pilot and Jack's secretary to be readily available. If he needed to come home quickly, I wanted everything in place.

"Thanks Rach." Jack took a deep breath and Emma untangled him from her arms as he stood. The world seemed to rest on Jack's shoulders as he looked out the window. Daniel Saunders' health had been failing for a long time. The speed at which the cancer spread had caught us all by surprise, and had caused the business to go into Jack's keeping earlier than expected. Despite having almost two years to prepare for his impending death, none of the Saunders family or staff was dealing with it well.

Jack gave his shoulders a shake, settling the weight across them evenly and standing taller. He kissed Emma on the cheek and gave me a smile before heading to the helicopter pad on the far side of the house. Emma watched him walk away, her lips pressed together as he rounded the corner and disappeared from sight.

"How are you doing?" Emma asked. She stood behind me, looking out the window, with her hands on my shoulders. "I know you and Daniel are close."

I pressed my palms into my cheeks and placed my elbows on the table. I was trying to ignore the horrible ache in my chest. Daniel Saunders was the closest thing to a father I ever had. He was the man I gave a card to on Father's Day. He was the one who listened to my worries and ideas. He wasn't just the father of my boss; he was my friend. The thought that I was going to lose him terrified me.

Emma rubbed my back gently, small soothing circles as I swallowed down a sob. She didn't say anything, just kept the comforting circles going on my back. I didn't want to cry. Crying meant it was real and I didn't want that. Emma gave me a small squeeze.

"Never mind, then," she said. I could feel her bright green eyes studying me for a moment. "Would you like some good news to cheer you up? I've felt strange telling anyone with everything going on, but I think it might make you feel better."

I nodded, concentrating on her voice. An uneasy tension permeated the house since Daniel took to his bed. It took an incredible amount of energy to keep walking on the invisible eggshells, and despite Daniel's pleas to lighten up, it felt sacrilegious to laugh or do anything normal with the death of a man we all loved looming over us. I decided I could use a little good news.

Emma's joyful grin infused her voice as she spoke. "Kaylee's pregnant."

My face split into a grin. Kaylee, Emma's older sister, had recently found love. Owen had been Jack's vice president of fuel marketing until he quit to be with Kaylee. I hadn't spent much time with Kaylee, other than at Emma's wedding and a shopping trip, but I had a gut feeling that she would be be a wonderful mother. I was more excited for Emma, enjoying her joyfulness at being an aunt.

"How is she handling it? Especially since she and Owen are running that bed and breakfast." It felt good to talk about something that didn't affect me.

Emma laughed. "Like she handles everything. Perfectly. She says the nausea isn't so bad, and Owen has been taking care of the bed and breakfast side of things. They are pretty much perfectly happy."

"Good. I like knowing someone is happy." I really liked the warm, fuzzy feeling knowing someone's world was working out the way it should. "When is she due?"

"Late April. They've known for a little while, but they wanted to make sure before they told anyone. My parents are so crazy excited. It's all they talk about now. I'm just nervous they are going to start asking me when I'm going to give the little bean some cousins." Emma's nervous expression at the future question made me smile.

"Yeah, when *are* you going to get knocked up? I want to be Aunt Rachel." I gave her an evil grin. I knew Jack and

Emma wanted to wait a little while to have kids, but it was too easy a target not to tease her.

Emma gave me a playful push, and we both giggled softly in the kitchen. It felt good to smile, if just for a moment. A new life was always something to smile about.

Footsteps entered the kitchen, and both our faces quickly schooled to reserved dignity. Emma turned and gave the source of the footsteps a welcoming smile, her shoulders relaxing as she recognized the intruder. I turned, and my shoulders tightened, butterflies suddenly dancing the mambo in my stomach. Seeing Dean always made my insides quiver like a teenage girl with a crush.

Dean stood nonchalantly in the doorway. His worn leather jacket hung casually across comfortable jeans, his lithe muscled body giving the fabric beautiful contours. He looked relaxed, but I knew he was always working. His light blue eyes were always active, his muscles ready for anything. He took his job as Emma's bodyguard very seriously. He gave us both a smile as greeting.

"Emma, will you be staying on the grounds for the rest of the evening? I saw the helicopter prepping and wanted to check with you." Dean gave his full attention to Emma. Since I was with Emma much of the time, it was often the three of us.

"I'll be staying here." Her eyes grew big for a moment as she realized something. "Has Jack left yet? I wanted him to drop something important off at the office."

Dean glanced at his watch. "If you hurry, you'll catch them. They're just finishing the flight plan and takeoff checklist."

"Thanks, Dean. I'll be back in a bit, Rachel," Emma said. She touched my shoulder as she stood to go catch her husband. I hadn't expected her to become such a close friend, but I loved having her around. She kept herself busy managing a wildlife rehabilitation fund, but she loved it and it allowed her to work on a regular basis with Jack.

Dean stepped out of the hallway to allow Emma to leave. She gave him a quick smile as she passed, hurrying up the stairs to fetch whatever it was she needed. I felt a quiver start in my stomach at the thought of being alone in a room with Dean.

"I heard about Daniel," he said, stepping back into the kitchen. "How are you doing?"

His blue eyes held genuine concern. I wished that he could just wrap me up in his strong arms and tell me everything was going to be okay. I wished that we could have a chance at being together, but I knew that just wasn't going to happen. For one moment, I just wanted my heart not to feel torn.

"I'm okay. It doesn't feel real. I keep expecting him to bounce down the stairs with a naughty grin and tell us all that it was just an elaborate, horrible prank." I gave him a weak smile.

I could see the hesitation in his body language. He wanted to come and comfort me, but we both knew that would be a bad idea. There was too much potential energy between us.

"Did Emma tell you about Kaylee?" Dean asked. I wanted him to leave so that I didn't have to think about him, but I also really just wanted him to stay. He took a step closer to the table, leaning his tall frame against the empty chair Emma had been sitting in. I could barely smell his cologne, masculine and clean, from here. My heart started speeding up in my chest.

"She did. You know Kaylee better than I do, but she seems like she will make a great mother." It still surprised me at how easy it was to talk to him. The few times we had been left alone together, Dean always outmaneuvered my initial awkwardness and made it easy to talk to him. The last time we had started talking like this, we ended up picking Emma up late because we lost track of time.

He gave me one of his notorious smiles and nodded. "She is going to be great. Owen too."

I brushed a strand of hair off of my cheek, suddenly feeling self-conscious about my appearances. I knew I shouldn't care, but I did. I wanted to say something incredibly witty and funny, something that would make him laugh and make his blue eyes sparkle. Just as I was about to speak, Dean's phone beeped.

"Excuse me," he said, clicking the headset in his ear. He stepped out toward the hall, leaving me with my thoughts. I may have watched his ass as he walked out, though.

I could hear him in the hallway as Emma came back into the kitchen.

"You should go talk to him," she said, sitting back down in her chair.

"Daniel's awake? I didn't want to disturb him."

Emma gave me an exasperated look. "Not Daniel. Dean."

"Why would I want to do that?" I tried my best to sound aloof, but I could feel a blush starting to warm my skin.

"Because, Ms. Blushy-Face, I see the way the two of you look at one another. I see the way his eyes gravitate to you when you walk in a room, the way you suddenly start blushing and fixing your hair whenever he's close. Anyone who knows you could see there is something between the two of you." She crossed her arms and gave me a look that dared me to deny it.

"Emma, it can't happen. The Saunders have a strict no-dating policy between employees. It's a clause in our contracts." *A clause Daniel made very clear to me when Dean was hired*, I thought to myself. I crossed my arms and gave her a equally stubborn look. She rolled her eyes.

"I'm sure Jack would give you an exemption from the policy if you asked," Emma answered.

"It's in every employee's mandated contract. That's not something that Jack can change without approval from the board of directors. Even if he wanted to, Jack would have to jump through some serious hoops to do it, with no guarantee that the board will even allow it." I fiddled with the pad of paper on the desk next to my computer.

Emma made an exasperated noise. "Rachel, it's obvious that the you two have feelings for one another. Screw the policy and follow your heart."

I turned slowly and gave Emma my full attention. "That is a sweet and romantic notion, but it isn't a feasible one. We breach our contracts, and we'd never be hired in this town again. My non-disclosure agreement would make it impossible for me to switch clients, and Dean's considered a 'loose cannon', especially after the incident protecting your sister in Dubai. If he was fired for messing around with the boss's personal assistant, he would be un-hireable, regardless of the reason. That's not a risk that either one of us is willing to take."

Emma pouted her lips. I knew she would be contemplating a way around our employee contracts, but I wasn't going to try and stop her. I hoped she would just forget the whole thing and let Dean and me handle this ourselves. Despite our "obvious attraction", what we were doing was working. It involved a lot of ignoring one another and simply making sure we didn't put ourselves in tempting positions. It had worked so far.

"Fine. I get it. You signed a contract, and losing your job

is a bad thing." Emma glared at me, but I held firm. This wasn't something she could change. It was how it was.

"Thank you. I know you mean well, but just leave it alone, please." I gave her a serious look. She sighed and nodded.

"I won't press it again. I'll let you get back to work. I'll see you at dinner, though, right?" Emma gave me a hopeful smile. I nodded. Everything was back to normal.

Emma wandered out of the kitchen, and I could hear the stairs creak as she made her way up to the guest room she used as an office when she stayed out here. I turned back to the computer screen, the blank page still mocking me. I closed my eyes, took a deep breath, and then tried to dive into my work and forget the way Dean's eyes crinkled when he smiled.

CHAPTER 2

*J*une 5*th*, 1990

AN OLD MAN walked by wearing a Speedo swimsuit that left nothing to the imagination. *You've got guts, dude,* I thought, and then snickered in my head. *Yup. You've got guts- and that's the problem!* The man continued to strut up the beach, but my eyes didn't follow him. I was pretending to read a book, laying on my stomach facing the ocean, but really I was just people watching. I had read the same paragraph four times and hadn't turned the page yet. The tourists were just too interesting.

Granted, I was a tourist too, but that wasn't going to stop me from people watching. My roommate, Jenny, nudged my beach chair with her foot, tipping her head toward the man who had just walked by. I peeked over the top of my Ray Ban sunglasses just in time to see him scratch himself.

"Thanks, Jenny," I said, sticking my tongue out at her.

She gave me a innocent smile and made sure the long brown hair in her side ponytail was still tight against her head.

"No problem, Rachel. I thought you would appreciate that," she said with a laugh as I rolled my eyes at her. "Even with a view like *that*, I am having a great vacation. This was a great idea, Kimberly."

Kimberly leaned forward on the opposite side of me and adjusted her big floppy hat with a satisfied grin. This trip had been all her doing. Her aunt owned a little vacation condo a few miles from the beach and was renting it to us three girls for practically nothing. Pooling our money together for gas, we had taken a road trip in Jenny's beat-up station wagon and were now enjoying a week of fun in the sun. It was the perfect way to celebrate our graduation.

"Hey, would one of you put some more lotion on my back?" I asked. "I think I can feel it starting to burn." I pulled myself into a sitting position and dug under the chair for the bottle of sunscreen. Kimberly opened her hands like a football player so I could toss the bottle in her direction. I pulled my long dark hair out of the way as she squirted the white goop onto her hands and began working it into my skin.

"Are you painting on her back?" Jenny asked, watching Kimberly draw designs into my skin with her fingertips. I didn't mind; it felt nice, and I knew she would rub it all in eventually. If she left it and gave me weird tan lines, she knew I would get her back.

"Just seeing a pattern in her freckles," Kimberly said as she traced a circle on my skin. I looked at Jenny and the two of us began to giggle. Kim was renowned in the art department for her abstract art pieces. She had a tendency to see things very differently. All three of us had just graduated from college with our Bachelors of Fine Arts degrees. I sported a new Fashion and Design specialty, Jenny was Marketing, and Kimberly had Drawing and Painting.

"You get me burned with one of your abstract designs, and I will put cockroaches under your pillow," I warned her. Kimberly laughed, but she hastily rubbed her design out and focused on making sure I didn't burn. Jenny snickered and settled back into her beach chair with her book. It looked like she was getting as much reading done as I was.

"There, all done." Kimberly patted my back gently, and I turned and gave her a smile. She was small and petite with light blonde hair and green eyes. She fixed the floppy hat on her head, then rubbed some extra sunscreen into her pale arms before handing the bottle back to me.

I settled back down with my book, glancing out at the waves. Blue water glistened along the shoreline. It was a quiet beach attached to a small town on the gulf side of Florida. The sand was white and fine, the waves soft and refreshing, and the town warm and friendly. It was probably going to be the last time the three of us would be together, now that we had all graduated.

"You get any responses on those internships?" Kimberly asked me. I shook my head.

It was kind of a sore spot for me. Kimberly had a job lined up in California. Jenny had an internship in Chicago. I had applied for several positions with designers in New York, Chicago, and even Paris, but so far I hadn't heard any responses.

"I talked to my aunt last night, and there haven't been any phone calls," I said. "She checked our mail, but all we have is an electric bill." I shrugged my shoulders. My senior design piece was created with a pregnant woman in mind, and while my professors loved it, it wasn't exactly what high-fashion designers were looking for. I had meant to make something that would appeal more to the industry, but the fabric had just sewn itself together. The dress had willed itself into being. At least I had gotten an A.

"You'll hear something soon. Your stuff is good. You know I wouldn't be able to get dressed without you half the time," Jenny said. I laughed. Jenny loved the flamboyant colors and patterns so prevalent in the current trends. She would wear so many colors it would make my eyes hurt to look at her if I didn't tell her to at least tone it down a little. Maybe not wear the flannel with the neon blue and pink patterned shirt.

"Well, at least I've still got my job at Charlie's." I tried to sound upbeat, but compared to my roommates' successes, it was hard to be happy about my art-supply store job. Neither of my friends said anything, but just gave me supportive smiles as we all settled back into quiet. The gentle murmur of the ocean shushed at our feet as we all pretended to read.

I turned a page, finally making it past that last sentence, when I saw *him*. He was tall. And handsome. And just a whole handful of *whoa*. I was very glad I had dark sunglasses, because I was most definitely staring.

Just down the beach, the most beautiful man I had ever seen was emerging from the water. His dark hair was cut short, and he ran a hand through it, sending a spray of crystal drops through the air. I could see every perfect muscle from my chair, his body lithe and lean. His muscles weren't bulky, but instead were toned and perfectly propor-tioned. A tattoo of an eagle with spears clutched in its talons screamed out from his delicious-looking shoulder.

He glanced over, and I felt my heart stop. His eyes peered right at me, and I could feel a blush starting to form as that Adonis of a man looked at me. I pretended to be very interested in my book, not wanting to be caught looking.

When I glanced back up, he was greeting two more perfect specimens of the male species standing at the water's edge. All three of them had the same tattoo on their respective shoulders and all three were drool worthy.

The three men walked casually down the beach and away from us. I was sad to see them go. They were so much better to look at than Speedo Guy. My beach chair shook as Jenny kicked it hard.

"Did you see those hot military guys?" she asked, excited.

"The ones with the tattoos? Yeah. Why?" I could hear the wheels turning in her head as she began plotting.

"I think the one with the dark hair was looking at me." She gave me a sly half-smile. *He was looking at me!* I wanted to yell at her, but it wouldn't matter anyway. For all I knew, she was right. He could have even been looking at Kimberly. "I think we should find them tonight."

"You're boy crazy," I told her with a roll of my eyes. She licked her lips, and I knew that tonight, we were going to be in for a man hunt. Jenny had a thing for men in uniform, and there was no way she was going to be talked out of having a good time trying to find them tonight.

"Yeah, but you know that you're going to benefit from it," she answered with a grin. "Besides, it's a vacation. We deserve a little something nice."

Kimberly groaned softly. I just shook my head at Jenny, but I knew we were going to have a good time.

CHAPTER 3

June 5th, 1990- Evening

THAT NIGHT, in the tiny beach town, Jenny, Kimberly, and I were dressed to kill. Jenny wore shiny black leggings that emphasized her dancer-like legs with a purple and gold shirt, while Kimberly chose some amazing acid-washed jean shorts with a neon green tank-top. I had on a hot pink mini skirt with an oversized teal t-shirt hanging off one shoulder. We had used up a bottle of hairspray getting ready, so our hair looked fantastic, despite the humidity. We were ready to have some fun.

We headed down to the main bar in town. It was called "The Pirate's Revenge" but everyone knew it as just "Revenge." Half of the venue was open to night air, music blasting out and the lights twinkling into the darkness. It was the place to be. Jenny giggled and grabbed my hand, pulling me urgently toward the welcoming lights. If those military boys were anywhere tonight, they were at this bar.

We stepped inside, adjusting our eyes to the revolving colored disco lights, and there they were. All three of them were leaned up against the bar, their jeans showing off perfect asses. Their t-shirts were ripped, and I could see how muscular they were underneath their clothing. One guy's shirt was a particularly bright shade of red and another had a gorgeous mane of blonde hair. However, "Blondie" and "Redshirt" weren't the guys that I was really checking out. The dark-haired one I liked was laughing at a joke Blondie had told. I did a quick check, and while there were no girls currently hanging on them, hungry looks abounded. We would have to move fast if we didn't want competition.

Jenny sidled up to the bar, wedging herself between a bar-stool and the dark-haired one who had been looking at me earlier. He turned and gave her a once-over, a cocky half-smile crossing his lips. The other two raised their eyebrows as she used her sexiest voice, though it was hard to hear over the music. "Hey, Soldier."

The handsome, dark-haired man set his drink down on the bar, careful not to spill it. Behind him, Blondie nudged Redshirt. They gave us appreciative smiles before turning to hear what the dark-haired man said to Jenny.

"Hey, yourself." The dark-haired man's voice was even better than I could have expected. I could have listened to him talk all day.

"Can I buy you a drink?" Jenny said, flirting shamelessly. I fought the urge to roll my eyes, especially since I knew she would be hitting Kimberly and me up for the cash later to pay for it.

"Of course," he said. "Whiskeys all around, then." He

grinned at her as he called to the bartender and ordered the house whiskey. I wanted to play in this game too, so I slid in between him and the blonde friend. Kimberly was hot on my heels.

"I'll take one too," I chimed in.

The dark-haired man turned and raised his eyebrows at me. I finally got a look at those crystal clear blue eyes of his. I could lose myself in those eyes. "You like whiskey?" He gave me that cocky half-grin, and I couldn't help but smile back.

"Make mine a double," I said to the bartender as he poured out a row of drinks. Mr. Tall-Dark-and-Handsome gave me an approving nod as we all reached for a drink.

"What are we toasting to?" Blondie asked as we raised our glasses.

"To meeting new friends," Jenny shouted right away. We all grinned, clinked our glasses, and drank. The amber liquid gave a satisfying burn as it went down, and a happy warmth starting to tingle in my limbs. This was going to be a good night.

Jenny set her empty glass on the bar. "I'm Jenny. This is Rachel, and that's Kimberly."

"I'm Dean," the dark-haired man said with a smile. His blue eyes twinkled in the dim light.

"I'm Matt, and this here's Anthony," Blondie added, tipping his head toward the tannest of the three.

"Call me Tony." Redshirt gave all three of us girls a big grin, but his brown eyes lit up when they met with Kimberly's. I could practically hear Cupid's arrow fly past me and skewer the two of them, even with the bar music playing overhead.

"So, Dean, where are you boys stationed?" Jenny asked, fluttering her eyelashes. I gave Matt a shy smile as I played with my glass, rolling it around between my fingers. He was big and tall; I guessed he had probably played football in high school given his build, and I would have happily had another drink with him, but his eyes were glued on Jenny.

"What makes you think we're stationed anywhere?" Dean said, leaning his back against the bar, able to see Jenny on his right and me and everyone else on his left.

"Your tattoos." Jenny brushed her hand against his arm where the eagle's claws poked out under his shirt sleeve. "I like tattoos. You wanna see mine?"

Dean stiffened slightly at her touch. It was as though he finally realized that she was focusing her attention on him, and that the rest of us were watching to see what happened next. He frowned slightly as he tried to figure out what to say without turning her down.

"Dean's not big on tattoos, but I'll show you mine if you'll show me yours." Matt jumped into the conversation before Dean found the words he was looking for. I hid a small smile as I turned towards the bar, looking for the bartender to order another drink. Matt's eyes hadn't left Jenny from the moment she walked in. There was no way he was going to let her walk out with anybody else.

Jenny looked Matt up and down for a moment, then glanced at Dean. A slow smile crossed her face as she realized she had a sure thing with the muscular blonde man. How did the saying go? "*A bird in the hand is worth two in the bush.*" It was almost magic as she shifted herself away from Dean and next to Matt.

"Buy me a drink?" she purred, oozing desire. Matt's face broke out in a goofy smile, and he waved the bartender over. The bartender actually paid attention to him, and scuttled back down the bar with two fresh beers.

Matt threw some money on the bar and wrapped his big arm around Jenny, leading her off toward a booth. I knew she was going to be having company tonight. I managed to catch the bartender before he disappeared again, ordering myself a beer.

"I guess that leaves just you and me," Dean said, putting money on the bar for my beer before I had the chance. I glanced beside me to see that Kimberly and Tony had vanished into a dark corner of the bar together. Looking at Dean, though, I wasn't sad. I was glad to have him all to myself.

"I'll get the next one, then," I said as the bartender whisked the money away before I could tell him otherwise.

"Deal." The man had a wicked grin. It was just lopsided enough to give him such a cockiness that I couldn't decide if I wanted to smack it or kiss it off his face.

"It was Dean, right?" I asked. I was doing my best to play nonchalant, but it was hard. With those blue eyes, and rippling arm muscles, he could have had me on the bar right there.

Dean nodded. "So, what are three lovely ladies doing in a town like this?" The corners of his eyes crinkled as he smiled and sipped on his drink from before we arrived.

"We just got out of school. We're celebrating while we still have loan money and before real life sets in. What about you?" I asked. It took conscious effort not to inch closer and touch him.

"We're on leave. We have to head back out at the end of the week." He said it like it didn't bother him, but his jaw tightened and his arms crossed his chest. I could tell that he wasn't looking forward to returning to whatever real life was for him.

"Why'd you come here?" I asked, guessing that if he didn't mention where he was going, he didn't want to talk about it. "I would think you would want to go to a bigger city for a vacation. Someplace like Miami or Vegas, not a tiny tourist-trap beach town like this."

He gave me that wicked smile again. Something deep inside me started to ache to feel that smile kiss me. I hadn't felt this physically attracted to a man in a long time. I'd had a couple of boyfriends in college, but nothing had ever really stuck. My relationships were either all physical or all mental, and neither of those will last for long without the other.

"Frontera's mom has a beach house here. It's nicer than anything we could have gotten anywhere else," Dean said matter-of-factly. "She's not using it, so we got it for the week. Besides, this place is all Frontera ever talks about. We had to make sure he wasn't making it up." He took a long draw on his drink.

"Frontera?" I asked, confused.

"Tony. Sorry, he's Anthony Frontera, but we usually call him Frontera."

"Well, I guess if you need to, you can call me Weber," I said with a smirk.

He laughed and finished his drink. "All right, Weber. What's your plans for your 'real life' that you're delaying by coming here?"

Normally I would have been put off by such a question, but I opened up to Dean immediately. I bought the next drink, and he bought the one after that. My head was starting to buzz, so I slowed down, feeling that I had drank enough.

I talked about my hopes of working for a fashion designer in New York, about my dreams of opening my own design place. In the meantime, how I'd be happy just to get a job in the field. He listened attentively, nodding at just the right spots, asking questions that I was happy to answer. It seemed so easy to fall into a conversation with him, and I felt myself leaning closer and closer as we talked. He didn't volunteer any information about his job in the Army, and I didn't ask. I was happy to talk about myself for a while.

After talking for what seemed like forever, I decided to change the subject. "So," I said with a sly smile. "Where is this house that Tony couldn't shut up about?"

"Are you trying to get my address?" Dean asked with a mock-scandalized look, putting his hand up to his face like some Victorian age lady. I couldn't help but laugh. "It's right off the beach and about half a block that way." He nodded his head up toward the expensive houses. "It's the blue one."

"Are you serious?" I exclaimed. "That place is huge! You could fit half the Army in that house," If it really was the house I was thinking of, it was the biggest house on the beach.

"Yeah, it's probably the nicest place I've ever been," he said. He set his empty glass on the bar and gave me that smile again, this time with a little bit of conspiracy behind it. "You want a tour?"

"Hell yes!" I couldn't even hide my excitement.

CHAPTER 4

*J*une 5th, 1990- Evening

DEAN TOOK me by the hand, and we stumbled out of the brightly-lit bar and onto the sidewalk. I knew that the other girls would wonder about where I went, but I didn't care. I could feel the whiskey and beer buzzing through my system, making me giddy. We were outside before I realized that Dean hadn't let go of my hand. I could feel his heat seeping into my skin, sending little tendrils of electricity up my spine. I was lightheaded, and I knew it wasn't just from the alcohol.

Since I'd seen the house while out on the beach with Jenny and Kimberly, I already knew the way to the house. I half-consciously started to lead the way. "What's your hurry?" he asked. "That eager to get me to my house?"

I stuck my tongue out at him. "All right, big guy, what else do you have in mind?"

He shrugged his shoulders. I couldn't help but notice the strength in them whenever he did that. "Have you ever checked out the shops in Old Town?"

I smiled. "Yes, we went there earlier today, as a matter of fact."

"Did you check out the surf shop? There was some surf-boards with some fantastic designs on them," he said.

I shook my head. If I had seen it, I had probably just walked right past it. I had never been surfing in my life.

He grabbed my hand and smiled. "Come on!" he said, sounding like an excited five-year-old. I couldn't help but come along.

When we got to the store, it was already closed for the evening. Still, Dean pressed his face to the glass and looked at them. Even in the dim light from the street, I could see a whole wall full of surfboards. Dean pointed out a few that he liked. The ones he picked tended to be simple and super masculine. The rest were mostly beach scenery, but one in particular caught my eye. It reminded me of a watercolor painting, something that Kim would have painted.

"I love surfing," Dean said, still peering into the store. "One day, when I retire, I'm going to live on some resort island and just surf every day." He turned toward me, smiling. "How about you?" he asked.

I laughed. "I have no idea where I'll retire. I have to actually get a job to retire someday."

He laughed back at me. "I didn't mean that. I meant surfing! Do you like it?"

I crossed my arms. "I've never been."

"Never been!" he shouted, as if he had never heard something so ridiculous. "I'd love to give you a lesson sometime."

I smiled. "I'd like that."

Our eyes were locked. Dean's crystal blue eyes seemed

to gleam as he delved into mine, and I just wanted to melt right into them. "For now, though, you wanted to see the house."

I fell out of the trance for a moment. "Right. The house," I said. He held my hand again and began to lead the way. Suddenly, he seemed to be walking a little faster, as if he had a purpose now.

It was a short walk to the big, blue house. As Dean stepped onto the Southern-style porch, I was just tipsy enough that I missed the last step and tripped. Dean caught me effortlessly, wrapping his strong arms around me and making sure I never hit the ground.

This close, I could smell his cologne. It was clean and fresh, like soap but with a super masculine undertone. His heat was wonderful against my skin, sending little pangs of hot desire deep into my core. His face came close to mine as he made sure I was steady on my feet. For half a heartbeat, I was sure he was going to kiss me. I wanted him to kiss me more than anything. Our lips were so close that I could feel his breath, and I leaned forward, silently begging him to kiss me.

But he simply gave me that infuriating smile and pulled away.

He didn't let me go until he was sure I was relatively stable, but I shot him an evil glare. I had wanted that kiss. He simply continued to give me that impish grin as he grabbed my hand and led me inside the giant house.

The inside was just as beautiful as the outside. The wooden floors creaked as we crept past heavy white wooden furniture with comfortable-looking cushions and giant painted seascapes to a big open kitchen. Dean let go of my hand for a moment. The disconnection almost seemed to cause me physical pain, even though he only did it to open the fridge and get us drinks. I wandered across the wooden floor until I came to a couch facing the large window overlooking the beach. The moon was starting to rise, casting a magical glow across the white sand.

I flinched as a purple and gold top went flying past my head, followed by a giggle. Looking down over the couch, I could see arms and legs of two people, along with the tattoo that we had heard Jenny admire. Color rushed into my cheeks. I backed away slowly, and Jenny and Matt never even noticed me, but I still couldn't get the blush off my face. I made my way into the kitchen where Dean grabbed my hand and hurried me to the foot the stairs. Moans of pleasure started to come from the couch, and the two of us giggled as we sneaked up the stairs. The dark seemed warm and inviting, caressing the two of us like clandestine lovers.

Dean guided me carefully down a hallway and into a room. He hit the light switch, and I instinctively closed my eyes as the light blinded me. When I opened them up again, I surveyed the room. The king-sized bed dominated the space, but the wicker furniture was comfortable-looking and reflected the easy style of the beach outside. Dean held up a bottle of champagne with two champagne flutes in one hand, condensation already collecting on the cold glass. He headed toward two big French doors.

He threw them open, the sea air filling the room as it came in off the ocean. I turned off the light, letting the soft glow of the moon transform the room into something romantic and wonderful. Dean set the glasses on a dresser near the doors, pointing the champagne cork out toward the water. The pop as he released it made me jump, the satisfying rush of endorphins making the night that much better.

With a delightful flair, Dean handed me a glass of the

bubbling golden liquid. I bit my lip with anticipation as he raised his glass in a toast, his voice warm and seductive in the moonlight.

"To meeting new friends."

"To meeting new friends," I echoed, my own voice somehow more sensual in the moonlight. The bubbles tickled my nose as I took a sip. The ocean air blew softly through my hair. Dean stepped closer, our bodies inches apart and yearning with need. He set his glass on the balcony, his hand then finding its way to the small of my back so that he could draw me in to him.

His eyes shone as if the stars themselves burned within. He leaned forward and brushed his lips across mine. The sensation made my spine feel like it was made of champagne, bubbly and ready to float away. I pressed my lips against his, begging for a better taste. He opened his mouth, the effervescence of champagne permeating my senses. I smiled as I moaned softly. All I wanted was to drink his champagne kisses.

Dean's hands flew all over me, touching me in places I hadn't been touched in quite a while. I felt the lust coursing through his body as he tugged at my shirt, and I wanted more. I wanted it so badly that I found myself jumping up and wrapping my legs around him before he even had the chance to remove my shirt. His hands grabbed me around the waist and held me up as we passionately kissed each other. My fingers went to the bottom of his ripped t-shirt, pulling it over his head.

There was that chiseled form that I had admired at the beach. He was muscular but not overly so. *"Strong"* was the word that I was searching for. He held me up with ease, his strong arms supporting me with no problem whatsoever. I reveled in the feeling of his chest, feeling those *strong* muscles. My fingers went to my own shirt, pulling that over my head as well. It wasn't long before I had my bra off as well.

Dean lifted me even higher. I ran my nails across his upper back and shoulders as his mouth went to my breasts, kissing them hungrily. He began to walk over to the bed, which required quite a bit of talent, since he had been drinking and he couldn't see where he was going. I squealed with laughter as his legs bumped into the bed and he slowly let me down. As I hit the sheets, I unwrapped my legs from around him.

I didn't waste a moment. I leaned up, undoing the belt on his jeans immediately. As I unbuttoned his pants and pulled them down, I saw the bulge in his briefs. I froze up while looking at it, and he chuckled and pulled his pants the rest of the way off.

He knelt in front of me, grabbing my leg in his hand. As his kissed traveled upward, I lay back down on the bed.

"I think I've died and gone to heaven," I said.

"Not yet," he said, kissing even further up my leg. When he reached the bottom of my skirt, he slowly hiked it up, bringing it up past my underwear. I had worn a thong, the first I had ever owned, and I already felt naked as soon as he could see it. He continued nibbling his way, tasting me, his lips touching every spot where the fabric ended and my skin began.

His tongue found my nub, and he began to lick over my panties. The alcohol still in my system made me lose control quick, and I found myself writhing underneath his touches immediately. I thought that this was as good as it got in life. That was before he pulled the fabric of my thong to the side, licking directly on my sensitive sex.

My world seemed to fall away from underneath me, and

I found myself quickly rising toward an orgasm. The way his stubble rubbed against me, the cool air of the night, and the steady and rhythmic pressure against my body drove me to the brink quickly. I grabbed onto Dean's head as I found myself falling off the edge, moaning as my orgasm took over my muscles, making them twitch with delight.

Dean continued to lick me, but then he stood up. The last piece of his clothes, his briefs, were off of him, and I marveled at his naked body in front of me. The V-line of his muscles headed toward his groin was simply spectacular. Truly, an Adonis stood before me.

He quickly pulled my skirt and thong off, then slowly moved on top of me, kissing me deeply. I could feel his manhood pressing against my inner thigh. He pulled the hair from my ear. "I want you," he said.

I shuddered with pleasure at his breath in my ear, and my eyes closed. "I want you too. Take me," I said. I felt him shift, felt him approach my opening.

"Wait!" I cried out, my eyes shooting back open. He looked at me with barely-contained lust. "Don't you have a condom?"

He hesitated. "Aren't you on the pill?" he asked.

I nodded quickly, and he seemed to take that as permission to continue. He moved even closer. I closed my eyes, and in my inebriated state, I almost let him...

"Stop, Dean. Put on a condom," I said.

He frowned, then smiled. "You're right, of course. I got a little carried away. Thanks." He immediately got up. I watched his muscular body walk across the room and root around in a nearby duffel bag. I definitely checked out his ass as he bent over to search. Finally, he pulled out a square package.

I smiled as I watched him unroll the condom onto his

fully erect penis. As he crawled back onto my body, I let him know just how I felt about his responsibility by spreading my legs even wider. I knew I was extremely wet; I had wanted this all night.

He entered my temple slowly, and I wrapped my arms around him as he filled me. He slowly pumped into me as he looked in my eyes, obviously searching for a sign that I was enjoying myself. I searched his face, biting my lip and writhing under his solid body.

I watched his biceps flex as he moved his body back and forth. His pecs hardened as he positioned himself for maximum pleasure. I even stole a glance behind him, watching that ass of his as he moved up and down, undulating like a snake. Everything about Dean turned me on, and when those piercing blue eyes met mine, I felt like I could melt there in his arms.

Suddenly, he grabbed my hips in his hands and rolled to one side. The bed was big enough that there was no way we could fall off, but I still screamed as I felt the butterflies in my stomach. Dean stayed within me as he rolled, and soon I was on top of him. I leaned up, intending to give him a show, but his strong hands went to my shoulders, pulling me back down on top of him.

He began to thrust upwards into me, and I was trapped against his muscular chest. He moved into me quickly, a grimace forming on his face. He started slowing down, as if he didn't want this to be over yet. He seemed to relax a little bit, as if he was backing away from his orgasm, and he let go of me so that I could take charge. I arched my back, grinding against him, giving him the most pleasure that I could.

The grimace returned, but he didn't try to stop me. Instead, he grabbed my hips and moved at my tempo. I watched as a light sheen of sweat formed on his skin. He locked eyes with me, and then he squeezed his eyes tightly shut. His strong hands gripped me even harder, and I knew I'd have a couple of bruises. I didn't care. I cried out louder than ever as I felt him jerk under me, finally finding release.

A few moments later, I stopped grinding. I felt myself falling onto his sweaty chest, putting my ear against it and listening to his racing heartbeat. His breathing returned to normal, and soon his heart rate slowed as well. I laid there, enjoying the feeling of this strong man underneath me. He pulled out of me, quickly tying the condom up and throwing it to the floor. His hands immediately returned to my back, his fingernails rubbing up and down my spine. Every touch from him sent tingles through me.

I raised my head from its place on his chest, and looked him in the eye. I had been in this position before, and I'd always felt embarrassed, like I should get dressed quickly. Not this time, though. This time, I felt like this was where I belonged. I felt like it was right.

Dean must have felt right too. "Hey, Rachel."

"Hey, Dean," I quickly said back to him.

"Would you go surfing with me tomorrow morning? The swells are supposed to be amazing on this coast," he said, sounding a little sheepish.

I smiled at him. "You mean you don't want this to be a one-night stand?" I asked.

He shrugged, then threw on a cocky grin. "I mean, I'm here for another few days, and I like you just fine."

I rolled my eyes. "I guess I'm around for a few days as well, and I like you just fine too."

He smiled and closed his eyes. "Good." Like tons of other men, it seemed like he was about to roll over and fall asleep.

I rolled off of his muscular body and snuggled up next to him, using his arm as a pillow. "Since I'm going to be surfing so early in the morning, I might as well spend the night here," I said.

"Might as well," he said. Then, he really surprised me. He turned toward me and gave me a kiss on the top of my head. A man had never done that to me.

We were both completely spent, totally sweaty, and closer than either of us had ever been with another person.

CHAPTER 5

 *resent Day*

HALF OF A TURKEY sandwich stared up at me, daring me to eat it, but I just couldn't find the appetite. I had eaten the first half, and had even enjoyed it, but my aching heart was taking up all the space in my body and I just didn't have room to fit the sandwich. I pushed the food away, the plate making a soft grating noise along the wood table.

The Saunders family portrait stared out at me from across the table. It was one from when the two boys were young. Jack stood next to his father, his hair neat and eyes bright. Robbie, his younger brother, sat on his mother's knee. Despite the outward calm of the picture, I remembered running around trying to catch Robbie to make his hair lay flat for the picture. He had run around the studio like a wild child, eventually tripping and scraping his knee. I could see the edge of the bandage poking out from beneath his shorts.

The table vibrated. I looked askance at the plate, wondering if I had angered the turkey sandwich gods by not eating it; I hadn't pushed it that hard when the tabled buzzed again. Shaking my head at my thoughts, I picked up my phone and the table stopped humming. It was a number I didn't recognize, but that was common enough with my work phone.

"Rachel Weber, how may I help you?"

"Hi Rachel. It's Robbie. I, uh... I need you to come get me." Robbie's voice crackled over the line. His words slurred together just enough that I knew he had been drinking. I sighed. When Robbie was on land, he was always drinking. Some days I was glad he was on his boat just because I knew that meant he was sober. Robbie had a strict rule that he never, ever sailed drunk.

"All right. Where are you? I'll send a car." If I knew Robbie, he was at the bar by the marina in a small town a couple of hours north of the Saunders' mansion. I had picked him up there more than once, to the point where the owner knew my car on sight.

Robbie stayed silent for a moment. "I'm actually gonna need you to come get me. Not just send a car." *Uh-oh.* This wasn't going to be an easy bar-run.

"Where are you, Robbie?" I managed to keep my voice even. Getting angry with him never worked. It was because I kept calm that he trusted me. There was a reason he never called his mother or brother to get him. It meant several three-o'clock in the morning phone calls, but at least that also meant that he always told me the truth.

"Winchester..." Robbie said. "in the county jail."

I closed my eyes and counted to ten. Some days I just didn't know what to do with him.

"Why are you in jail, Robbie? Please tell me it's for something minor." I had bailed him out a couple of times, usually for public intoxication or finishing a bar fight. He always finished a fight, even though he never seemed to start them. *Please let it be just a little bar fight...*

"I hit someone with my yacht. I technically had the right of way, but.." his voice trailed off.

"But what, Robbie?" I began rubbing my temple with my free hand. *Please, don't have killed anyone! Please, please, please...*

"I was drinking. That's why I'm in lockup."

Shock went through me like ice water. Robbie hit someone with his boat because he was drinking? But Robbie *never* drank and sailed. That was like saying he could breathe underwater. It just wasn't something he *could* do. The fact that he was drinking and sailing startled me more than if he had said he had accidentally killed them.

"You were sailing drunk?" I couldn't believe the words could even come out of my mouth. From the corner of my eye, I saw Dean step into the kitchen and pull the milk out of the fridge. I found myself focusing on his smooth movements, my brain refusing to believe what it had just heard and instead focusing on something it could understand. Dean carefully screwed the lid back on and put the jug away, leaning casually against the counter as he sipped on the glass. I could tell he was waiting for me to get off the phone, but I didn't care if he overheard my phone conversation. He knew all the trouble Robbie had been in up to this point.

"Yes. Listen, this is my one phone call. Will you please come get me? And don't tell Dad. He already thinks I'm a screw-up." Disappointment and failure rang through his voice. My heart sagged in my chest. Their relationship was difficult at best. Telling a dying man that his youngest son was in jail was not something I wanted to do.

"I'll keep it quiet. You said the county jail in Winchester, right?" I closed my eyes, trying to figure out how to get there without anyone noticing.

"Yeah. I know you'll worry about this if I don't tell you. The sheriff hasn't told anyone I'm here yet, so you don't have to worry about that. He said he'd keep it quiet until you got here. The girl I hit is at Mercy Hospital." Robbie's voice somehow sounded more dejected. "And the girl... I hit Sam, Rachel."

"Sam? Samantha Conner?" I opened my eyes as another shock hit me. This was going to be a rough afternoon.

"Yeah. Will you check on her?" Robbie asked. He sounded devastated. Samantha had been his best friend until she moved away when he was thirteen. He had been heartbroken when she left. I had lost track of her, but he had obviously found her again. Unfortunately, it was with his boat.

"Of course I will. I'll be there in a couple hours, all right?"

"Yeah. I'm really sorry about this, Rachel." He somehow managed to sound even more forlorn.

I sighed. "I know, Robbie. And I want you to know that I'm pissed. I'm coming to get you, but I am *not* pleased." Even through the phone, I could hear him shrink. I was one of the few people whose opinion mattered to him.

"Thank you, Rachel. I really mean it. I don't know what I'd do without you," he said. His voice was quiet.

"I'll be there soon." I hung up the phone and pressed my palms into my eyes. This was not what I needed today. What I needed today was a massage and a glass of wine.

"Who's in jail?" Dean asked, sliding into the seat next to

me. He set his glass down with a quiet click on the table. I glanced over, his blue eyes full of concern.

"Robbie. He was sailing drunk. I have to go bail him out," I answered. I folded my hands under my chin, looking out at the leaves and trying to think. I had to go get him without raising suspicion. I knew Emma would cover for me but that Jack would be furious if he found out. There was no way I was going to let Daniel know, though.

"I'll go get the car." Dean stood smoothly, picking up his glass and heading toward the sink.

"What makes you think you are coming? Robbie asked *me* to come get him. And... and you're supposed to be watching Emma." The idea of being in a car with Dean, alone, for two hours had me simultaneously excited and terrified. I wanted desperately to be alone with him, but frightened of what could happen.

Dean gave me a level look, his blue eyes capturing mine. "You're going to want my help."

"Why? I can drive myself, and I've bailed Robbie out of jail before. This isn't a new thing," I scoffed at him.

He set the glass in the sink and stepped closer to me. He came close enough that I could smell his cologne, his face only inches from mine. My fingers itched to reach out and touch him while my stomach did flips worthy of the Olympics. I had a sudden wish that he would just lean over and kiss me.

"You need me." He gave me one of his crooked smiles. "I know the sheriff in Winchester. He owes me a favor. Wouldn't it be nice if Robbie didn't have this on his record?"

With him this close to me, I was having trouble concentrating. I just wanted to touch him, to kiss him again. Even after all this time, I still dreamt about that last kiss. I needed to focus on something other than his perfect lips. I smoothed the top of my head, making sure it was still in a tight, neat bun. *Be professional. You can't have him. He probably doesn't even think of you like that anyway.*

"Fine." I said, narrowing my eyes at him. "I'm driving though."

His crooked grin widened to a full out smile, his eyes twinkling. *And I'm thinking of kissing him again.* This was going to be a long day.

CHAPTER 6

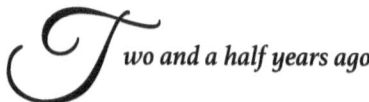

wo and a half years ago

Bianca Saunders strode toward me with anger flashing in her eyes. I froze in my seat, quickly forgetting the memo I was typing. She should have looked demure in her dress suit, gold flowers shining out happily from a field of silver, but instead, she just looked like an angry bee. I hoped I wasn't the one about to be stung.

"Jack needs a new bodyguard." She threw a newspaper at my chest as she stomped across my office and into the executive lounge, heading toward the coffee pot. She tottered on her golden heels, shaking in her rage and splashing coffee across the counter. Some of the dark liquid spilled on her jacket, and she cursed under her breath as she grabbed a napkin and began dabbing at the silver and gold embroidery.

I fumbled with the newspaper and groaned slightly when I saw the headline. **Billionaire's Bodyguard Assaults**

Photographer blazed out in bold letters across the heading of the page. In a blurry black and white photo, Jack looked on in horror as his bodyguard's massive hand reached for the photographer. Every word in the article made me cringe; the lawsuit from the photographer was going to be huge.

"Jack was caught leaving his girlfriend's, or who I assume is his girlfriend, apartment. Instead of having a car ready, or having Jack go out the back, this buffoon has him walk right out into the photographers and then throws their cameras on the ground. He then punched one of them for asking a question." Bianca pinched her nose with her thumb and forefinger, her brows tightening. "The photographer is already suing. We don't need this kind of publicity. Especially not as we start the process for Jack to take over the company."

The article ended with a question about Daniel's failing health and the speed at which his son was taking over the company. Jack wasn't supposed to take control of the company for another three years, but it looked like he was going to have to start much earlier. I didn't want to think about the fact that the results from Daniel's biopsy were coming in today. I carefully folded the newspaper back up and tipped it back toward Mrs. Saunders. She waved her hand, dismissing it, so I set it on the desk. The older woman sipped on her coffee, the caffeine seeming to calm her, at least temporarily.

"The current one is just a giant walking slab of meat. He doesn't have a brain in his head, and this latest incident just pushes the point home. This is the third photographer that is suing us this year. At this rate, they'll just start lining up at the front door for us to hand them money." Mrs. Saunders sighed. "At least that would save us the lawyer fees."

"Do you have any preference as to whom we hire? I can

ask around the agencies..." I started, already thinking of whom I could call to get a bodyguard with a brain. Bianca's anger disappeared as she realized I was willing to get a new bodyguard. She had been expecting a fight, and now that there wasn't one, she relaxed. I knew Jack liked his current guard, but he needed someone that had a brain to go along with the muscle, and we both knew it.

"No need. I have someone who comes highly recommended." Bianca smiled at her efficiency. I smiled, but inwardly I winced. Bianca, while a shrewd negotiator and intrepid businesswoman, was not known for her hiring skills. She was the one who had hired the current bodyguard, against my recommendation.

"What kind of experience does he have?" I waited, hoping he at least had some.

"He's military trained. War hero with a bronze star. He was working in Hollywood for some actress, but he's available now. He comes with a recommendation."

"That sounds promising," I said slowly. I narrowed my eyes and looked at her. "Why is he available now?"

Bianca blushed slightly and fidgeted with her cup. "Well, he got into some trouble and was fired. But he was fired for protecting his client too well, not for using his giant meat claws. He really does come highly recommended."

"Recommended by whom?"

"The girl's manager, Don Renalds. He hated getting rid of him, but the girl insisted. From everything Don said, this guy will be perfect to keep Jack safe as he takes over the company."

I sighed and chewed on the inside of my lip. I didn't like putting Jack's safety in the hands of a stranger, especially one who was recently fired. The Saunders were the closest thing I had left to family, and I would be damned to see Jack under-protected.

"What did he do to get fired? Details, please."

Bianca gave me a confident smile. "The girl has a substance abuse problem, and he was keeping her dealers away."

"I can see why she would fire him and her manager want to keep him." I sighed and pushed my hands together, trying to think. I had met Don a couple of times, and he seemed to have a good head on his shoulders.

"I know you don't like it when I jump into Jack's personal matters," Bianca said, setting the cup of coffee down behind her. She put a hand on my shoulder and smiled. "This man is available now. Hire him. If he doesn't work out, it will give us enough time to find a replacement, but at least it will be better than what Jack has now. Please, Rachel?"

"Fine. I'll give him an interview. If I don't like him, I'm not hiring, though." I gave her a serious look. Mrs. Saunders picked up her coffee and beamed at me. She was back to being a peaceful gold and silver meadow.

"I wouldn't expect anything else. I think you'll end up loving him." She smiled, pulled a card out of a pocket, and handed it to me.

I read the small embossed name on the card, and my heart stopped. *Dean Sherman.*

"Are you all right? You look like you've seen a ghost," Mrs. Saunders asked, looking concerned. I swallowed hard, my mouth suddenly dry.

"No, I'm fine. I just remembered something is all. I'll set up an interview right away." I hoped she couldn't hear the tremor in my voice. I hadn't seen him in over twenty years, but just reading his name brought back the memories of him as though it was just yesterday.

Mrs. Saunders nodded and began walking out the door. I stared at the card in my hand for a full five minutes before working up the courage to call the number and make an appointment.

CHAPTER 7

*J*une 6th, 1990

I WOKE up nestled on Dean's arm, using it as a pillow. We were still in more or less the same spot that we had had sex in a few hours before. He was snoring softly, which was really cute. I looked at my watch and found that it was still really early. My head was swimming a little bit and I really had to go to the bathroom. I didn't want to wake Dean, so I tried to sneak out of the bed. However, my hair must have tickled his arm, because his arm shot out and grabbed mine. He took me by surprise, and I squealed a little bit. He laughed.

"Where do you think you're going? We're supposed to go surfing," he said, obviously still half asleep. He blinked, then let go of my arm. His eyes focused, and he looked me up and down. I blushed. The sun's light was much more illuminating than the moon's, and I realized that he was drinking in his first clear sight of my naked body. This man was a stranger, and suddenly I felt extremely self conscious. I pulled the sheet from the bed up to my body, covering my breasts.

He smiled at me. For a moment I thought he was going to pull me back into his bed. Instead, he jumped out on the other side. Last night hadn't been a dream-- his muscular ass was as hot now as it had been the night before. I dropped the sheet, partly in surprise. Everything about his body screamed physical fitness.

Still, I didn't want to get too awestruck. He had seemed charming and intelligent last night, but that could have been the alcohol talking.

"I should probably get back to my place," I said. He looked at me like he was hurt for a moment, and I realized that he really wanted to take me surfing. "I have to get my bathing suit," I continued.

He relaxed and smiled. "Yeah, absolutely. I don't think my spare would fit on you too well." He fished out a pair of trunks out of an olive duffel bag and threw it on the bed.

"Plus, I'd have to go topless," I added with a laugh. "No way I'm wearing this bra in the water."

He looked me over again. "I wouldn't mind," he said, clearly doing another once-over on me.

I blushed and quickly pulled my clothes on from last night. They smelled like cigarette smoke, even though I didn't even remember anyone smoking near us the night before. Still, I had to get home somehow. Dean watched me the whole time. "I'll be back in half an hour," I said.

"I'll have breakfast ready for you." He gave me a charming smile.

I grinned at his thoughtfulness and walked out his bedroom door. In the front room, I clearly saw the purple and gold top still crumpled on the floor. I looked over and saw Jenny and Matt passed out on the couch together. Jenny was still on top of Matt and practically drooling on him. I thought about waking her up but then remembered how long it would take her to get ready, particularly if she were as hungover as I thought she'd be.

I whistled the whole way back to our little condo. I hadn't had sex in months, and the night before had been the best sex I had since... well, maybe ever. Even with the bruising on my hips and the mild hangover, I felt better than I had in a long time.

I entered the condo, expecting that Kim would be worried sick about the two of us. I came in and smelled eggs cooking immediately. Kim was in the kitchen in her comfy pajamas, humming as she cooked. When she turned around and saw me, she smiled. "Hey, there."

"Hey, yourself," I said.

"You hungry?" she asked.

"No... aren't you wondering where Jenny and I were last night?" I asked.

She shrugged. "Tony saw each of you leave."

I had forgotten all about Tony, and shrieked a little when a masculine voice came from behind me. "It's important to have situational awareness."

There, sitting at the table, was Redshirt, only he wasn't wearing the red shirt anymore. He was just wearing a pair of boxers, comfortable as he could be. Normally I would be pretty worried about such a good-looking guy practically naked at our table, but I had just walked out of a house with his two naked friends.

I giggled. "You startled me!"

He laughed back at me. "Did you girls have a good time?"

"Yes, I had a blast. In fact, I'm meeting Dean right now to go surfing," I said.

Tony looked past me at Kim. "Hey, do you want to go surfing?"

Kim blushed and looked down. "Actually, I was kind of hoping we could stick around here today. Together."

Tony shrugged his shoulders. "That sounds good to me. Let the guys know not to trash it too badly."

I smiled at him. "I thought you loved that place; why aren't you rushing back to it?"

Tony shrugged again. "They don't cook eggs for me there?"

I laughed and went upstairs. I ran a shower and stepped in to rinse off. Without even thinking about it, I wished that Dean was in there with me. I wanted his strong hands on me, touching me and washing me. I smiled to myself at such an intimate a thought.

After I was done, I found the bag with my swimsuits in it. For a moment, I agonized over which to wear, the one-piece or the two-piece. If I wore the two-piece, the top might fall off if I crashed into the water too hard. On the other hand, it was sexier than the one-piece.

You're only young once, I thought. I quickly put on the two-piece bathing suit, slipped a pair of short shorts and a t-shirt over it, and was on my way back to Dean.

CHAPTER 8

June 6th, 1990

"OKAY, now this time I'm going to just give you a little push on the back of the surfboard. Center yourself and get ready."

We were out in the ocean. Dean was taking the time to show me how to surf and it was not going well. As he gave my surfboard a little tap, I found myself staying up on the surfboard for about a half second before crashing into the water again. *Oh well*, I thought. *At least my top is still on.*

I came to the surface, sputtering once again. Dean grabbed my hand, steadying me before going after the surfboard. He grabbed it and brought it back to me.

"Quick, get back on the board, I can see a great swell coming," he said, obviously excited.

"You take it." I unlatched the surfboard from my ankle and handed him the strap. Dean had seemed excited about surfing, yet he hadn't even gotten on the board yet.

"Please, just ride this wave. Then you can watch me surf for the rest of the afternoon," he said, pushing the strap away.

I laughed. "Okay." I laid on my stomach, waiting for his signal.

"Okay, on the count of three, stand up. One, two, three!" I felt the push on the back of the surfboard and stood up. The wave began to carry me away, and I managed to keep my balance. *This is it*, I thought. I was actually traveling over the water, standing as the wave behind me pushed me toward the shore.

I screamed a victory scream as I felt the exhilaration overcome me. Then I made the mistake of looking back at Dean. I quickly lost my balance and fell off the board, crashing into the water with an ungraceful somersault. I came to the surface, coughing but cheering too. Dean was there in a minute, holding out his hand for a high five. "You did it!"

I reached out to reciprocate the gesture, then started to go after the board. In a moment, my feet brushed the bottom. We had hit a sand bar, and the water only came up to the middle of my chest. I kept walking toward the shore, but Dean's hand reached out and grabbed me. I stopped to look at him. "What's your hurry?" he asked, wrapping his other hand around my waist.

"But... your surfboard..." I started.

"It'll wash up on shore," he said, then leaned down and kissed me. I quickly lost myself to the kiss, wrapping my arms around the back of his neck. His hands went to my sides, pulling me in closer. As we stood there, kissing, another wave crashed against Dean's back. My feet lost their grip on the ocean floor, but Dean stayed steady. I wrapped my legs around his hips. He was a rock that I could cling to, and as another wave hit us, I found myself gripping him even tighter.

The salt water tasted delicious on my lips as the two of us kissed, and I was getting more turned on by the moment. My chest was heaving, and as another wave splashed into us, I held onto him, my breasts pushing against his muscular pectorals. My hands moved down his neck to his back. My nails dug in, grasping for purchase as his hands moved down to my ass.

I broke from the kiss and looked behind me. Anyone on the beach would have to really squint to see us way out here. I turned and faced Dean. His blue eyes looked at me, then looked over the top half of my body hungrily. I smiled as I lifted my bikini top off of my breasts. It still hung off my neck, though. There was no way I was going to let my expensive bathing suit drift off into the ocean, especially knowing that I'd have to make it back to shore to get my shirt on.

Dean removed one of his hands from my ass, bringing it up to my boobs. His strong fingers kneaded them. Every time his hand touched my nipple, I felt a surge of pleasure rush through my veins. I could feel the bulge in his shorts as our bodies rubbed together. I wanted it. I wanted him more than I had ever wanted anything before. As our kisses grew more intense, I moaned loudly. I was working myself into a frenzy, and there was nothing I could do to stop it.

Dean wasn't much better off. My moaning seemed to be spurring him on, and he growled hungrily as he moved his lips to my jaw. As he moved his mouth farther down, his teeth grazed the skin of my neck before he nibbled my shoulder. My nails clawed at his back, and I meant to scream out "Dean!" but it came out as only a whisper. He heard me loud and clear, though, and he kissed across my neck to my other shoulder. He bit down on that one too, claiming me as his own.

I had had enough and couldn't take any more. I moved my hands down, tugging on his shorts. I felt him pull his rod out, pushing it against the fabric of my bikini bottom. Without a second thought, I pulled the fabric to the side, allowing him access to my inner sanctum. He pressed against me...

And then he pulled back. He looked at me very seriously. His blue eyes searched mine, asking for reassurance. "I don't have a condom," he said sheepishly, his mouth forming half a smile. An unanswered question lay behind those eyes. *Are you okay with this?*

All thoughts of rejecting him were already out the window, but that last gesture was the moment I knew I was in love. To answer his non-question, I grabbed onto his manhood, guiding it into myself. A wave splashed on Dean's back, pushing him forward just as I felt him swell within me. His hands went to my ass, steadying me.

As he regained his footing, he began to move me back and forth. I couldn't help myself as I began to moan loudly. I glanced down to see him biting his lip, admiring at my body up and down. I felt so sexy in front of him, completely unashamed of any flaws I might have. I could tell that he thought I was perfect, that I was everything he wanted in a woman.

Despite wave after wave crashing over our bodies, Dean's pace remained constant. The friction against my body caused my own pleasure to rise and fall in waves, though it grew ever higher. Within another minute, I found myself hugging Dean's strong body tightly. Maybe if I held him close, he'd never stop admiring me, never stop causing me this pleasure.

I felt a tidal wave of euphoria rising within me, and I knew that it would soon crash against my shore. I held on for dear life as Dean's speed increased gradually, pushing me closer and closer to the edge. I felt my levee break, felt my body open up as ecstasy swept me up in its power. As my orgasm hit, I pushed myself away from Dean's body. I wanted to see those blue eyes.

Suddenly, Dean's fingers tightened on my ass. His face contorted but his eyes never left mine. I nodded fiercely, letting him know what I wanted. *Do it, please.* I was no longer thinking rationally, and as his mouth dropped with pleasure, I felt him fill my body with a tidal wave of his own. My own orgasm heightened, and I felt my muscles draw him in deeper. I wanted him. I wanted all of him, and I never wanted this moment to end.

The moment did end, though, and soon his pace slowed down. He stared into my eyes, his face full of wonder. I probably had the same look on my face, and the thought on both of our minds was clear. *How did we get so lucky?*

We kissed softly, tenderly, as the waves continued to crash over us. Eventually, he set me down. I fixed my bathing suit and he pulled his back up. He held my hand as he surveyed the beach for his surfboard. When he found it, he pointed it out to me, then squeezed my hand. He dove into the water and headed toward the beach. I followed close behind, realizing we hadn't said a word since our mutual orgasm. We didn't have to.

TONY AND KIM were still at the condo when we got back. Dean stayed in the front room and chatted with Tony as I changed out of my bathing suit. When I was naked, Dean entered my room. I began to cover up with my hands, but then smiled and relaxed. He still looked at me hungrily, as if he were seeing me naked for the first time.

"Frontera and Kim are going to stay here tonight," he said. "Would you like to stay at my place again?"

I smiled at him. "I'd love to."

"Bring some pajamas," he said. "I wouldn't want you to get cold."

DEAN and I laid on the roof of Tony's house. There wasn't much light pollution, so Dean told me about all the constellations he knew. He told me stories about being in the Army. I didn't care what he talked about. All I cared about was the fact that he was holding my hand.

Beneath us, Jenny and Matt were going at it again, and Jenny couldn't help but be loud. I was glad she was having such a good time, because I had never had a better time in my life. A shooting star flared across the sky, and I knew what my wish was immediately. I wished that this week would never end, that Dean and I could stay up on this roof or hang out at the bar forever. I'd even spend forever surfing with him.

If this vacation couldn't last forever, if life demanded that we move on, then I would be all right with that, as long as Dean was still a part of my life.

CHAPTER 9

Two and a half years ago

I ALTERNATED between staring at the heavy wooden doors and glaring at my watch. A notepad with a new pen sat waiting at my fingertips, but I wasn't even tempted to doodle. Dean Sherman had my complete and utter attention, and he wasn't even in the room yet.

What would I say to him? *Hi, Dean. I sent you a letter every day for a month, but I never got one from you.* That sounded too harsh. Especially since I knew he had never gotten a single one of my letters. I had sent them out religiously once I moved to New York to work for the Saunders family, but after a month of no replies, the postman had handed me a stack of unopened letters. Something in the address Dean had given me had made them undeliverable.

You could have just told me you weren't interested. Instead I waited for you. I asked my landlord to forward all my mail, but I never got anything. Not even a postcard! No, that wasn't fair either. It was very possible that my landlord just was lazy and threw out all my mail instead of forwarding it. Maybe he wouldn't even remember me. Maybe he had simply wanted to forget me.

Maybe I was just a stupid summer fling. That one hurt more than I wanted it to. Even after all this time, I still felt a connection. I hoped it wasn't just me.

The heavy wooden door swung open, and Dean strode in. My heart jumped into my throat as I took him in. It was definitely my Dean. He was still tall and lean, with the grace of a hunting cat. His dark hair had a slight smattering of silver, but instead of making him look old, it made him look distinguished. His eyes were exactly how I remembered them, blue pools the color of a winter sky.

He stopped for a moment as the door swung shut behind him. His eyes went wide for a moment, his cheeks going pale, but he regained his composure so quickly I wasn't one hundred percent sure I had even seen him hesitate.

"Hello, Dean," I said, proud that my voice didn't shake. I wiped my hand on my skirt under the desk before rising and offering it to him. His hand enveloped mine, the touch sending electrified tingles down my spine. His face gave nothing away as he let go and took a seat across from me.

"Rachel. I didn't know you worked for the Saunders family." He kept his voice neutral and professional, but I felt a thrill that he recognized me. I pushed my excitement down, though. Nothing good could come from it.

"Yes. I've worked for them for over twenty years. I'm Jack Saunders' personal assistant. I see you brought a resume?" I hoped I sounded confident because my knees were shaking. Dean slid a professional-looking resume across the desk. I had its twin in front of me, but I read down the paper again.

Joined the Army at seventeen. Selected for Special Forces and trained extensively. Deployments with Desert Storm and other classified missions. Released from the service and became a close protection officer in several diplomatic parties. His most recent position was with the young starlet.

"What made you choose this profession? It looks like you were a soldier," I said looking up at him over my glasses. He was sitting perfectly straight, his suit hanging in tailored clean lines off his lithe body.

"I was injured. I took a bullet to the shoulder which makes using a rifle painful. I was released with full honors, and my commander recommended me to the protection detail for a visiting senator. My skill set transferred easily, and I have been a close protection officer ever since." His voice never fluctuated. He was the perfect example of calm. I prayed he didn't see how nervous I was.

"I see. It appears as though you have ten years experience in this sector. Why are you looking for a new position?"

Dean shifted slightly in his seat. His jaw tensed for a moment, but he answered matter-of-factly, "I was fired for breaking my client's associate's nose."

I raised my eyebrows. He continued.

"My former client is currently, and publicly, seeking treatment for substance abuse. I believed the man in question was selling her said substance, and as per my contract, I stopped him. My client was not pleased and revoked the contract."

His honest admission surprised me. *You have been dealing with too many business sharks,* I told myself. I liked the honest and straightforward tone of his voice; the way he spoke with authority and self-assurance. He had grown up from the cocky young man and replaced it with real confidence.

"I see. If you take this job with Mr. Saunders, you will be required to sign a non-disclosure agreement, as well as have some strange hours. Mr. Saunders will need to have you at his disposal day and night. This is not conducive to a family life. Would this be a problem for you?" I hoped my attempt at finding out if he ever married wasn't too blatant.

Dean cocked his head for a moment, then gave me a sly smile. I blushed, knowing he had figured me out.

"I don't have any family. My parents died before I joined the service, and I've never been married." A sadness crept into his eyes. "I could never find anyone willing to put up with me. Do you find it hard to be in the Saunders' employ?"

I shuffled the papers on the desk before answering. I wanted him to know I was still single, still waiting for someone, without being obvious. "No. The Saunders are the only family I have. I'm married to my work."

A ghost of a smile crossed Dean's rugged features. The room was far too warm for my taste, and I felt a trickle of sweat run down my back. The electricity in the room was humming as though we had never been apart.

"I see you were with the one-oh-one unit for another two years after..." my voice cracked slightly as I remembered that vacation we had together, " after your deployment for Desert Storm."

"And?" Dean's eyes grew hard. I didn't know if it was from remembering our time together or what he had seen in the war.

"What happened to you?" *Why did you never write? Why didn't call me? You broke my heart!*

"I got shot. I watched my friend die in my arms and almost lost another. And the worse part was that we weren't even allowed to tell our families where we were. Frontera died and I didn't even get to tell his mother why," Dean said.

His voice stayed quiet, but there was a hidden anger and silent pleading for me to understand. He didn't write me because he couldn't. It didn't take the pain away.

"Tony died? What happened to Matt?" I couldn't help but ask. I wondered if Kimberly knew. She had always said she knew something bad happened to him.

Dean's blue eyes met mine. There was a dark pain in their cerulean depths and I wished I could jump up and hug him, but I knew I couldn't. It had been a long time since we were lovers.

"He's alive and well. He actually lives not too far from here in a little town on the coast." He watched me absorb the information. I waited for a moment to see if he would ask about Kimberly and Jenny, but he stayed silent.

I cleared my throat. This interview was getting away from me. "Why would you like this job?"

He flashed me a dashing smile and leaned back slightly in his chair. "I'm the perfect person to protect Jack Saunders. I'm subtle. I stop things before they happen. Mr. Saunders is the world's most eligible billionaire bachelor, and as a result he has the press's interest. His younger brother catches the media's attention on a regular basis, and thus thrusts Jack Saunders into the spotlight. He needs someone who can react and assess, and thus prevent a situation rather than smashing a reporter's camera."

"And what makes you think that's what I want?" My voice came out far huskier than I intended and I hoped he didn't notice the blush threatening to consume me.

Dean leaned forward, making my heart skip a beat as he came closer to me. "I know you want me because I'm here interviewing. If you didn't think I would be a good fit for this position, I wouldn't be here."

I swallowed hard. I stammered and began to fuss with

the documents in front of me. Dean gave me a smile and sat back, enjoying my fluster.

"Would you have any trouble reporting to me as your supervisor?" I asked the question bluntly, trying to find a way to regain control of the heat coursing through my body. With him sitting within arms' reach, every memory of our time together was flooding through me. I hadn't expected it to be like this.

"You are in charge, ma'am. I'll do anything you wish." He shot me a confident smile that made me unsure as to whether or not he intended the double meaning. The emotions of the past were threatening to overwhelm me, and I had to stop this before I lost control of the situation.

"You should know that there is a strict no fraternization between employees policy."

"That's not going to be a problem, *Ms. Weber*."

The room suddenly dropped ten degrees. I wasn't hot anymore. His face regained a guarded expression, the teasing grin gone. It almost hurt to have the tension between us cut so quickly. I wanted to fix it, but I knew I couldn't. Not if we were going to work together. Our past was very much over, and there was no hope for our future.

"Well, Mr. Sherman, you have all the necessary qualifications. This interview was merely a formality. The Saunders family had already decided to hire you. You start tomorrow morning. I'll have someone bring in the paperwork."

I stood up, my heart alternating between pounding and freezing. I didn't know what to do with the mix of emotions running through my mind. Dean stood as well and shook my hand. I could still feel the current of electricity running through our touch, though it didn't match with his icy demeanor.

Gathering my papers, I scurried out the door, afraid to

even glance behind me. I needed to clear my head and hopefully figure out what I was going to do. Working with Dean was not going to be easy, and I only had until tomorrow morning to figure out how to do it. *At least this time I wouldn't have the distraction of waking up in his bed,* I thought.

CHAPTER 10

*J*une 7th, 1990

THE SKY WAS JUST BEGINNING to glow with the promise of morning when I felt Dean slip out of bed. He padded quietly on the floor, picking up his clothes and dressing. I peeked one eye open to watch him wriggle into a pair of jeans and a t-shirt, admiring the view. It was worth it to wake up a little to see his body move. His blue eyes caught me peeking and he came over and sat on the edge of the bed.

"Go back to sleep," he whispered, leaning over to kiss my forehead. His lips were warm and soft, so soft that I never wanted them to leave.

"Where are you going?" Sleep made my voice creak like an old door. Dean brushed the hair off my forehead, smiling down at me. He looked like an angel in the morning light.

"Boy things today. Remember?" Dean's blue eyes twinkled with excitement. I nodded slowly, remembering that he had said something about going out with Matt and Tony today.

"Have fun. When will you be back?" I asked, sitting up slightly.

"Late afternoon." He kissed me again softly. "Go back to sleep."

I mumbled an "Okay" and shifted to my side, finding a cool spot on the pillow. Dean made sure the sheet was tucked up around me before he quietly tip-toed out and shut the door.

THE ROAR of motorcycle engines in the late afternoon made me look up. The growling rumble was loud enough to hurt my ears as three bikes powered up toward the house. Kimberly flashed me a big grin, practically flinging her book down on the sand in order to run to the front of the boys' house to greet them. I marked my place and grabbed my swimsuit cover. Then, I followed her at a more sedate pace. Jenny was already hot on Kimberly's heels.

In the large driveway of the big beach house, the three men revved their engines and grinned at us girls coming to greet them. Jenny hopped on the back of Matt's bike and squealed with delight as he raced around the open street.

Tony and Dean started doing dangerous-looking patterns with their bikes, obviously showing off their skills. The two of them made tight figure-eights around each other, eluding one another and certain death by mere inches. I wanted to cover my eyes, sure they were both going to crash and die. Then, they powered into a high-speed circle. They chased one another in such a tight spin that it looked as though their bikes were moving along the ground on their wheel rims. My breath caught in my throat, fear threatening to choke me.

I wanted them to stop. I hated motorcycles. Something about them scared me. Maybe it was the noise, maybe it was that I liked some steel between me and a certain death, maybe it was the accident that put my cousin James in the hospital for three weeks. In any case, to me, they were just glorified death traps.

Dean laughed as Tony pulled out of the circle-chase and over to where Kimberly stood, her hands on her face in total amazement at their daredevil antics. The manly testosterone effects of the bikes were certainly working on her and Jenny.

"Wanna ride?" Tony asked Kimberly, her shy smile threatening to beam off her face. She nodded and he pulled her onto the back of his bike, revving the engine. He handed her his helmet, and she kissed his cheek before putting it on.

"Hey, Hot Stuff," Dean said, giving me a wicked grin as he took off his helmet. "Hop on."

I hesitated for a moment. I didn't want this.

Dean raised his eyebrows waiting for me to answer. I could feel everyone's eyes on me, ready for me to join them. *It's just a motorcycle. They aren't going to do anything too dangerous. He isn't James,* I told myself. Besides, I trusted Dean.

The two other bikes took off down the drive, and Dean kept his hand outstretched. "Come on, it'll be fun!" he said.

"Promise me you'll stop if I ask you to," I said.

He looked at me like I was being a worry wart, then brought his hand up to his opposite shoulder. "Tap my shoulder three times and I'll stop immediately," he said, tapping his shoulder three times.

I bit my lip and nodded. I accepted the helmet from his hand and got on the back of the motorcycle. The bike shook like an angry volcano beneath me, and I clung to Dean for dear life. He was my rock, his abs hard and tight under my arms as I pressed into him. I tucked my feet up and held my cheek into his back, squeezing my eyes shut as he cranked the engine.

With a terrifying surge, the bike jumped forward, the engine roaring in my ears. My entire body was vibrating, and I wished my fear would turn into excitement. I wanted to like this. I wanted to impress Dean with my willingness to do exciting things. I wanted to be like Jenny; I could hear her laughing and begging Matt to go faster. I opened one eye to see the two of them nearly parallel to the ground in a deep turn as they were about to turn onto the road. The image made my stomach flip, and I quickly buried my face into Dean's back. *Please, please don't do that to me, Dean*, I begged in my head.

Dean turned, his body weight shifting to guide the bike. I clutched desperately at his shoulders, praying that I wouldn't hit the ground. I clung to his back like I was drowning in fear. James had spun out on a turn. This was not fun. With every turn, the ground seemed to rise up to meet me, promising a painful fall. All I could see was my cousin's body in the hospital bed with the white bandages and tubes going into his arms. The scars up and down his body from where the road slowed him down.

"I want off, please," I whispered. I was surprised I made any noise at all. Every fiber of my being wanted off that bike. Dean must not have heard me, the whistling wind stealing my words before they reached his ears. Instead of slowing down and letting me off, the bike increased in speed. I opened one eye in time to see Matt and Jenny rush past. I wanted to scream. The three boys were horsing around, weaving in and out between one another on the empty street like it was a game. I felt the breeze as Tony and Kimberly whizzed by, their engine screaming in my ears. I never wanted something to end so badly.

"Let me off!" I finally screamed, beating at Dean's back. I knew it wasn't quite the code that he had given me, but he took the hint quickly enough. He pulled the bike to the side of the road, stopping as quickly as he could while still being gentle. He turned around, his cocky grin fading as he saw the terror on my face. I scrambled off like the bike was molten hot. The helmet was suffocating me, so I ripped it off and let it drop from my fingers, backing onto the crab grass of the front lawn, my palms sweaty. I wiped them on the thin blue fabric of my swimsuit coverup. I couldn't decide if I was burning hot or terribly cold. My knees wobbled, and I only stayed standing by sheer will power.

"You okay?" Dean's brows knitted together, confusion and concern etched on his face.

"I don't like motorcycles," I said. I concentrated on breathing in and out. In and out.

He hesitated for a moment. "Okay, then we'll go do something on our own," Dean said. He looked back where we had come from. "I have to drop the bike back off at our house. If you get back on, I'll go really slow."

"No." The idea of getting back on made me want to throw up. James's voice echoed through my head, the moans of pain any time he moved calling out from my memory.

He sighed, then held his hand out. "I'll take the helmet, then. Wait here and I'll be right back." I leaned forward and picked up the helmet. Dean took it from me and winked before putting it back on. "Don't get on the bike with those other guys. They're crazy."

That finally made me smile. Dean's engine growled to life and he took off. I watched him go, my hands still shaking a little bit. Still, I was happy that he listened to me. Within a few minutes, Dean was jogging back up the road to where I was at.

"I'm sorry," I said immediately. "I know you wanted to ride your motorcycle."

He just shrugged. "I did that already today." He took my hand in his, pulling me gently to start walking with him. We traveled quietly for a moment, away from the house and the motorcycle.

"I'm sorry I freaked out on you like that," I said quietly. Dean just nodded as the tension between us broke. He didn't say anything. "My cousin and I were really close. He was in a really bad motorcycle accident last year."

Dean gave a quiet "mmm-hmm" and squeezed my hand.

"He was in the hospital for three weeks. The doctors said he was lucky to be alive, but he was never quite the same after that. I've never liked motorcycles since."

"I'm sorry I pushed you, then," he said softly. "You doing better now?"

I nodded and rested my head against his shoulder. He felt good against me. I bent my arm behind me, pulling his hand so that it wrapped around my waist. My world felt right again.

CHAPTER 11

*J*une 7th, 1990

THE BOARDWALK CREAKED under our feet as we made our way along the sandy planks. Small local shops had their doors open to let in the warm ocean air and passing customers. The smell of hotdogs and popcorn drifted by, and music played softly from the inside the shops.

"I'm starving. You want something to eat? My treat." Dean let go of my hand, eyeing the food stand.

"Sure. I'll take a hotdog. Thanks!" I flashed him a big grin as he hurried over to the line. I was about to follow him, but something caught my eye.

On the edge of the boardwalk, facing out toward the ocean, a street vendor was selling his paintings. They were amazing. The seascapes caught my attention, particularly one of a storm about to roll in. A woman stood silhouetted in the foreground, tiny against the powerful thunderclouds and swelling waves. I could feel the surge of the water, the light fading quickly into the clouds as the storm threatened to overcome her. Despite the storm, she stood strong and ready to survive. I stood mesmerized by the play of colors and the use of light, exploring the nuances of the art.

"There you are," Dean said, coming up behind me. "I turned around and you were gone. What are you looking at?"

He handed me a hotdog, ketchup and mustard in clean lines down the middle. I pointed to the painting that had captured my attention.

"This painting is spectacular." I stepped closer, almost forgetting about the food in my hand. The painting was small, about the size of a hardcover book. I could see it siting on a bookcase or a mantle. I could also see the price tag and that it was more than my meager budget could afford.

Dean peered at it, tipping his head to the side as though a different view point would help. He shrugged and looked back at me. "What's so special about it? It looks like just another beach scene to me. There are hundreds of stupid beach vendors hawking this same picture all over."

I rolled my eyes. "No, there are no vendors with this painting. I've never seen one like this before, and I've been looking. I have a degree in art; I know this stuff. This is really good."

Dean gave me a skeptical look, biting into his hotdog. I turned back to the painting and began to point out the features.

"See the light here? How it contrasts with the dark of the sky and the water and silhouettes the woman? It's called chiaroscuro. Rembrandt is the artist who made it famous. But see how the sun shining on only this area creates a sense of forbidding? You can feel the storm coming, but she stands defiantly against it." I glanced over at Dean, and he had his brows furrowed, his concentration completely on the painting and me.

"I see it," he said, his voice quiet as he stepped toward the painting.

"See how the light and the dark interact? Without the light shining here, the dark wouldn't look so deep. The sun shining on her, making her a silhouette, in addition to her stance, is what makes her feel so strong. She is in the light despite the oncoming darkness. It is the way the two interact that make it powerful, the way the painter used the light to detail the shadows."

Dean looked over at me, his eyes filling with understanding. "I've never had anyone explain a painting to me like that before. I always just thought art was just kind of a bunch of glorified nonsense."

I gave him a smile. "Art is supposed to make you feel something. To help you experience the world. A good piece of art will change the way you look at things, maybe even change the way you look at yourself."

"Do you always see the world this way?" He gestured to the painting. "A world of light and dark and all the shadows in between?"

"Mostly. It takes a little training to get good at it, but I've always looked for the beauty in the world. That's why I went to art school. I love seeing the beauty in things that most people just take as everyday or ordinary."

Dean stared at the picture for another moment. I took a bite of my hotdog, enjoying watching him suddenly realize the beauty in the painting. I remembered the first time I really "got" a painting, and watching him was a wonderful mirror of that memory. The same slack-jaw stare, eyes wide, shoulders relaxed except for the one arm reaching out to touch the picture, but stopping before contact.

"You're right. It *is* beautiful," said Dean, turning to face me with a sheepish grin. "Thank you for showing me that. You like your hotdog?"

I hadn't realized how hungry I was, I had snarfed the entire thing down already. I pulled my finger out of my mouth, sucking off the last little bit of ketchup. I looked at him sheepishly, then we both laughed. "They're probably all waiting for us back at the house," I said.

We headed back down the boardwalk in contemplative silence. It was comfortable to just walk with Dean, knowing both our minds were still back with the painting. I could still see the whorls of color in the water and the light reflecting off the waves. Glancing over at Dean, I knew he could see it too.

CHAPTER 12

June 8th, 1990

WHEN I WOKE up in bed again with Dean, it was the first time that I didn't feel like things were perfect. This was the last day that I would spend with Dean, and I knew that none of us girls were ready to say goodbye. If there was ever a time when I felt at home, it was here in Florida, with my two best friends and the three guys that made us happier than we had ever been.

Still, when he rolled over and smiled at me, I couldn't help but grin back. "Hey," I said.

"Hey, Beautiful," he said. He looked completely at peace.

I turned on my side to face him. The sheet was down around my waist, and my breasts were exposed in front of him, but it seemed like it had been forever ago that I had any modesty around him. "What do you have planned for today?"

He shrugged. "I was hoping I could hang out with my girl," he said with a grin.

I beamed. *My girl*. The words sounded perfect coming out of his mouth.

"Well, yeah, but what are you going to do with *your* girl?" I asked, putting the emphasis on "your."

He shrugged again. "There's a volleyball net outside that we haven't even used. What do you say we go buy a volleyball and try it out?"

I smiled. Just the thought of Dean out there, shirtless, and using his strength in a masculine sport turned me on. I immediately thought of the movie *Top Gun*.

"You and me? One on one? I'm tall, but I don't think I'd stand a chance against you," I said.

"Well, bring your friends. Maybe we'll do guys versus girls; maybe we'll do couple against couple. We'll have to see how they feel about it," Dean said.

I smiled. "I'll head over to the condo to get the two love-birds while you go find a ball and let Matt and Jenny know."

"Oh, so you're going to make me brave the crazy sex room. *Thanks*." Dean made a face at me and we both laughed. Despite the heavy walls, we could hear the two of them going at it like sex-crazed monkeys. I shuddered to think of what he might find in their room.

We both got out of bed and dressed in the same room. I liked how comfortable we were together, even naked. It made me feel like it might last.

I tried to banish that thought from my head as I walked in the sunshine to the tiny rental. *This is just a summer romance*, I thought. I sighed. I wanted it to be so much more.

When I walked into the condo, I began to laugh. There were Kim and Tony, in their pajamas, a steaming mug of coffee next to each of them as they played checkers on the kitchen table. "Here we are, on a tropical vacation, and you two are indoors playing a board game. You look like an old married couple," I said.

Kim blushed, and Tony grinned unabashedly at me. I could practically read their thoughts. *We wish we were a married couple.* I wondered if he had proposed to her already. I heard guys often did that before a deployment. I'd have to get the info from Kim later.

"So, what's up?" Tony asked.

"We're about to start a game of sand volleyball at your place. Are you in?"

I could practically see the competitive side of him as he smiled. He looked over at Kim. "Can we pause this game?"

She smiled. "I'd love to." Her eyes sparkled. I didn't think that I had seen that smile leave her face since this vacation started.

"Okay! I'm going to go ahead and grab my stuff so that it's all over at my place," Tony said.

Kim was silent. Finally, something that made the smile fade from her face. She, too, realized that the vacation was coming to an end, and that it was time to disentangle themselves and their things. Soon, there would be no casual mornings full of checkers and coffee.

My heart hurt for her for a moment. All three of us girls would soon be wishing this summer never ended.

"ALL RIGHT, we're playing Shirts and Skins, right? Guy team will be shirts," Matt said, smiling at each of us.

"Matt!" Jenny cried out.

"Okay, okay... I guess we'll be Skins, then," he said. He smiled at the other guys as he pulled the t-shirt off his head.

The other two quickly followed suit, throwing their shirts to the side of the sand volleyball court.

My jaw dropped. I thought I saw Jenny swoon a little bit. I hadn't seen them all together in nothing but their bathing suits since that first day on the beach. Their bodies were all tight and muscular and their matching tattoos gleamed in the sun. I had to check my mouth to make sure I wasn't drooling. The men began to preen and flex for us a little bit. Matt even kissed his huge bicep and pointed at Jenny, winking. She rolled her eyes, but I knew that she was thinking what I was thinking. We couldn't pay for a better show than this.

The girls and I were looking good too. Jenny had opted for just her bathing suit. Kim and I had come in jean shorts and tank-tops, but I had taken my mine off and thrown it to the side, revealing my bikini top.

"I don't know, guys," Dean said. "Should we go easy on them?"

"I haven't gone easy on Jenny since we got here," Matt said.

A chorus of *oohs* sounded around the court while Jenny blushed, but she quickly regained her composure. "I guess if that's the best you've got, I should have no problem beating you at volleyball."

Both guys cracked up, and it was Matt's turn to look flabbergasted. "I'm going to make you eat those words, both on this volleyball court and later tonight."

"Bring it, big boy. First to fifteen points wins," Jenny said.

We hit the ball back and forth for a while to warm up; then the boys graciously let us start. Unfortunately, Jenny smacked the ball directly into the net on her first serve. "That was a practice! The game hasn't started," she said. She recovered the ball and sent it flying through the air. It came down fast- and all three guys watched as it landed right in the middle of them.

"I thought you had it!" Dean said, slapping Tony in the chest.

"Don't look at me! You should have backed up and got it!" he yelled.

Meanwhile, on our side of the court, we were cheering like we just won the state championship. When Jenny had the ball back, she yelled, "All right, boys, it's one to nothing." She did the same high-in-the-air shot. This time, Dean dove underneath it, just in time to bump it high enough for Matt to spike it over the net. None of us girls had a chance to react. We regretfully rolled the ball under the net back to the boys.

"Zero serving one," Matt said. He did an overhand serve, just inching over the net, but allowing the ball to drop right down into the sand before any of us even realized it was going to make it. We were no longer cheering.

That was basically how the next eleven points went. Sometimes we got it back over the net, but they managed to react quickly. There was a lot of high-fiving on the other side of the net, though, and that made me smile.

"Twelve serving one," Matt said. He sent the ball gracefully over the net, and Jenny bumped it up. I hit it, and sent it sailing over the net. Matt, then Tony, then Dean did a perfect bump-set-spike, but I was ready. I jumped at just the right time and slammed my fist against the ball as hard as I could. Dean and I both fell backward onto our asses, and I couldn't see anything but the sky above. From the sounds of the high-pitched cheering behind me, though, I knew what side of the net the ball had landed on.

Dean was over me in a moment, his big hand reaching down to help me up. I smiled as I grabbed it and he lifted me effortlessly to my feet. I looked into his eyes as we smiled at each other. Then, he swatted at my ass. "Good game, buddy," he said, and everyone laughed. I laughed too, then grabbed the ball and got in position for my own serve.

"One serving twelve," I said. I used to love volleyball in high school, and I'm sure I surprised them a little when I did an overhand serve myself, aimed squarely at Matt. With no time to react, he hit the ball up in the air and way out of bounds. The game was back on!

"Two serving twelve," I said when I had the ball back. I did the same serve, but this time Matt was ready. He bumped it, and Tony spiked it. Dean followed up with three serves that we weren't able to return, and the game was over.

"Who wants to go up against Kim and me?" Tony yelled.

"I do," Dean said. I stood up and got on the court. "Whoa, whoa, where are you going, Rachel? I want Matt to be my partner."

I laughed and kicked sand at him, and he charged me. I shrieked as he picked me up and threw me over his shoulder. He ran around, whooping like an idiot. When he set me down, he gave me a big kiss in front of everyone. "Guys, I've made a mistake. I want Rachel to be on my team. You guys can be shirts, we'll be skins."

I laughed again. I loved to see him having fun with everyone. I ran over to his shirt and buried it in the sand, then pulled it back out, making sure it was completely coated with the uncomfortable grit. "I think we should be shirts, come put it on," I said, sticking my tongue out. Matt was laughing so hard that I thought he'd fall off his lawn chair.

Dean shrugged. "I'll just take yours," he said. He ran over to where my tank-top was and threw it over his head. He didn't even try to get it over that massive chest of his, instead just putting his head through the top hole and letting it hang down around his neck. It only went halfway down his muscled torso.

"I'm ready now," he said. Everyone was shrieking with laughter now, including me.

"Zero serving zero," Dean said, and shot the ball right at Tony. Tony reacted quickly and got the ball to Kim, who sent it back over the net. I bumped it up, and Dean spiked it. The game progressed like that, Kim and me playing second fiddle to the match-up of Dean versus Tony. Still, I had a lot of fun. Dean and I ended up winning fifteen to five, mostly because Kim made some mistakes, but I could tell she was having fun. When the game was done, Tony swept Kim off her feet. "I don't feel like I lost at all, because I got the trophy right here!"

We played game after game of volleyball, winning some and losing some. Since I was the tallest girl, our team won most of the ones we played. We told jokes and bantered with one another, and I laughed until my abs hurt. My smiling muscles felt like they were going to fall off my face from all the grinning. It was the first time we had all really hung out since the night at the bar.

CHAPTER 13

June 8, 1990- Evening

AT SOME POINT when it started to get dark, Tony and Kim sneaked away and started a small fire down on the beach while the rest of us were on the volleyball court. Tony put some hamburgers on the grill that his aunt kept in the garage, and by the time we were done with the last volley-ball game, he had paper plates full of food for us to eat. We opened a bag of potato chips. Tony removed the grill from the fire and began to throw more and more fuel into it, quickly turning it into a bonfire. We cracked open some beers and all began to eat. None of us spoke much, busy eating and simply enjoying the good company.

I sat on the sand and watched the fire as the sun finished setting, leaning my head against Dean's shoulder as we munched on potato chips. The waves crashed against the beach below, and soon a cool wind began to blow in from the ocean. Dean graciously slipped my tank top off his neck and let me have it back. It was just the right amount of clothing to be comfortable, especially since it was still warm from Dean's skin.

This is our last night together, I thought with a heavy heart. I sipped my beer and leaned closer to Dean. On the one hand, I wanted to enjoy our last night together in bed, hopefully giving him something to look forward to upon his return. On the other hand, I was so comfy here. Dean felt solid, a rock for me to hold on to, and I didn't want to let him go for anything.

Jenny finally spoke up. "This has been some week, hasn't it?" Everyone muttered an agreement. "This is basically the best vacation I've ever had. To meeting new friends," she said, raising her beer in the air. It was the same toast we had shared in the bar. That seemed like a lifetime ago, and so much seemed to have changed since then. Still, I raised my beer in the air and clinked with Dean.

Jenny drank the rest of her beer in one swig. "I'll definitely be sorry to see you all go, but summer flings can't last past summer, can they?"

There was silence. Everyone but her seemed to be thinking the same thing, that they wished this summer could go on forever. The silence went a moment too long, and Jenny cleared her throat. Even Matt seemed to reel for a moment, but then broke the tension. "Yeah, if I had you for any longer, I'd probably break you in half."

Jenny smiled and laughed. "You were a pretty good lay, Grinswald, maybe the best I ever had. You take care of yourself." She was either oblivious to the fact that she was breaking Matt's heart, or she wanted to make it clear to him that what happened on vacation stayed on vacation.

Matt laughed but his voice sounded sad. "Same to you, Jenny."

Nobody seemed to have much to say after that. After finishing their beers, Kim and Tony took off back to the condo. Jenny whispered something in Matt's ear, then flicked her tongue against it. He smiled and nodded. The two got up and walked toward the house.

"Guess it's just you and me," Dean said.

"Guess so," I said. I didn't want this to end. I'd do anything to keep this vacation from ending. I hoped he didn't look at my face, because I was beginning to cry.

"Was I a pretty good lay?" he asked.

I laughed a little. "Maybe the best I ever had." Then I looked at his face, and he could definitely see the tears reflecting the fire's light. "Definitely the best I ever had."

He smiled back at me, his blue eyes seeming to twinkle. They were unquestionably wet. "That's encouraging," he said.

I laughed. "That's not what you're supposed to say," I said.

"What am I supposed to say?" His voice was soft and low.

I paused. "What if I asked you not to leave?"

Without hesitation, he said, "I have to leave."

"I know, but what if I asked you *not* to go? What if I asked you to come with me to a place where summer never ended?" I asked, my voice trembling a little bit.

"You have your own dreams, Rachel. You'd have to leave those behind," he said.

"I could deal with that." I was dead serious. "What do you think?"

Dean didn't answer right away. He hugged my shoulder and pulled me in closer. "There's something I haven't told you, something that you should probably know."

The tone of his voice told me that this was something big. *He's married*, I thought.

"I'm not just going back to the army base tomorrow. Well, I am, but it's temporary," he said.

He's got three kids, and he lives off base, I thought.

"There's a war going on right now between one of America's allies and a much larger army. They have no chance of winning without our help. So we're going to help." He paused. "I'm going to help."

I looked at him, suddenly feeling tiny and lost. "What do you mean?"

He sighed. "I leave for Saudi Arabia in three days. Our whole company is. We're going to be there in case the Iraqi army won't leave Kuwait."

I was shocked. "You're going to war? Why didn't you tell me?" I asked.

"Because this is a vacation. Because I didn't want to think about it. Because I thought that you wouldn't want to hang out with me if you thought of me as a trained killer instead of as a pretty face." He smiled, but it was an empty smile.

I laughed. "Don't be ridiculous. I never thought of you as a pretty face," I said. I started to laugh at my own joke, but I couldn't. Instead, I began to bawl openly, leaning into his shoulder. I didn't want him to go anywhere, and I certainly didn't want him to go to war.

Dean let me cry, stroking my hair gently. The fire began to go out in front of us, having consumed all the fuel that had been put into it. My heart felt the same way. In one week, I had known such intense highs that my heart had burned like a star, and now that it was starved of fuel, I felt it being extinguished.

I moved my head from Dean's shoulder. He tried to hide it as he wiped a tear away, but I knew. I looked at him. The dying light of the fire was just enough for me to see those crystal clear blue eyes. "Make love to me, Dean. Make love to me like this is the last night we'll ever spend together."

Dean nodded, then moved in to kiss me. There, on the beach where I first laid on eyes on him, the two of us became as one. I cried as I spent the last night I figured I might ever have with him.

Before that, I had never felt that close to anyone, and in the twenty years since then, I never did again.

CHAPTER 14

wo Years Ago

I SAT IN MY OFFICE, typing on my laptop. In a few short hours, I would be free for the weekend. Jack and his secretary, Brandi, were on their way to the Caribbean, and I was going to have a few days off. It felt wonderful to know I was going to have a weekend for myself. Things at work had me running overtime. Jack was about to transition to CEO of DS Oil and Gas, now that Daniel's failing health was making it harder for him to work. We had hoped to delay the transition another year, but Daniel's cancer was growing more aggressively than expected. The doctors were only giving him maybe another year.

I shook my head, ridding myself of the negative thoughts. I was going to have a weekend to myself. I had reservations at a charming little bed and breakfast in upstate New York, complete with a spa and relaxation package. It was going to be a great weekend.

My phone buzzed on the desk, and I picked it up. I frowned as soon as I saw it was Jack. He was supposed to be on a plane right now with his ditzy secretary, not calling me. I picked it up.

"Rachel, we need a new flight plan. And, we're going to need you to come to the airport and get on a plane," Jack said.

"What?" I was apparently now going on a flight. My weekend plans started waving goodbye.

"Oh, and will you please make a note to give Dean a bonus? He's been fantastic today."

"Sure. What's going on, though?" I felt like I was trying to put a puzzle together without the box. For some reason, Jack's flight plans were changing and I was now getting on a plane. And something about that all occurring meant that Dean was getting a raise.

"Somehow, the paparazzi were tipped off that I was going on a trip. Dean knows how important it is that they don't figure out where I'm going. This is my last vacation, and I won't have their busybody cameras ruining it." A touch of anger came into his voice, but he took a deep breath and continued. "When they followed us, Dean eluded them. We missed our original flight plan, but Dean came up with an idea. We're flying separately now."

"Okay. So I'm guessing Dean's going to fly with you, making it look like one of your business trips, and I'm flying with Brandi to make it look like a separate business trip," I reasoned out.

"You and Dean must share a brain or something. Dean and I are going to take the chopper into the private strip in Tampa. You and Brandi will take the jet. Once Brandi and I are safely on the jet together and on our way to the island, you and Dean can head home." Jack sounded very pleased with his little plan. I had to admit that it would get the paparazzi off his back, but there was just one small hitch.

"So you're going to make me take a plane ride with Brandi?" I made sure that my distaste was apparent.

Jack sighed. He knew I didn't like her. The blonde-haired secretary was a bimbo. A bimbo that I highly suspected was just after Jack's money and fame. She was pretty and did her job well enough, but I had a feeling that she would do whatever it took to get into Jack's wallet. And right now, that was pretty easy because she was already in his pants.

"I know you don't like her, but this is my vacation. I wanted her to come along," he said quietly. I could tell he was muffling the phone so she wouldn't hear.

"No, I don't like her. I think you can do so much better. She's a gold-digger. I wish you would just find someone with a brain in her head."

"Unfortunately, I don't exactly have a lot of opportunities to meet women. We can talk about this later. Right now, I want this to get underway. Dean already has the helicopter en route. He wants me away from these paparazzi as soon as possible, so we'll be in Tampa before you." Jack switched on his business voice, telling me that it was time to do my job.

"Yes, Mr. Saunders. I'll be right there."

I MANAGED NOT to kill Brandi. I was close, though, especially as she filed her nails for the billionth time and blabbered on about her "designer shoes." I kept it to myself that they were obviously a knock-off and that they gave her clown feet. I hoped she broke a heel stepping in the sand with them. Longest three hours of my life.

When we finally landed, I practically skipped off the plane. Jack walked sedately up the private tarmac, greeting me as I came out.

"You owe me a raise," I told him sweetly.

"Like you don't already have access to all my bank accounts already," he responded with an eye-roll. I gave him a grin.

"Have a great time. I'll do my best not to call you, but I make no promises." I gave him a quick hug. "Be sure to compliment her shoes."

"Her shoes? I don't understand women and their shoes. I need to find someone who likes just wearing sneakers. Sneakers I understand." Jack's eyes glazed as he looked up at the plane and thought about shoes. I had a sneaking suspicion that this fling with the secretary wasn't going to last long. I hoped he still managed to have a good vacation anyway.

Jack waved as he stepped up the metal staircase to the cabin door. He looked like a movie star as he ducked inside. I walked quickly off the tarmac and into the small office, pulling out my phone to figure out how I was going to make it back. With any luck, I could catch a charter flight home and still make it in time for check-in at the B&B.

One new message. The green light blinked on my phone. I decided to listen to it before making my flight plans. Maybe Dean had waited with the helicopter and I wouldn't have to worry about planes at all.

"Hi, Rachel," a male voice slurred. "This is Dean. I'm gonna need you to come get me."

The message ended abruptly as though he had dropped the phone. I stared at my cell for a moment, at a loss as to what to do. I couldn't believe he had called me.

I had tried to avoid him as much as possible since his

having been hired. It had been easy enough. The few times that I had been alone in a car with him we had been polite and civil. Since we were usually just waiting for Jack to arrive or emerge from a meeting, our encounters had been thankfully brief. It appeared to be working.

I thought I was over the heartache of losing him. We only had a few short days together, and then he had never written me any letters. Despite his promise to come find me, he never did. I had forgiven him a long time ago, but now, with the Florida humidity and his voice still in my ears, I was having a hard time.

Dean was the one who got away. I had tried to have boyfriends since he left, but they never lasted long. They were either only looking for a way to get to Jack Saunders, or they weren't content playing second fiddle to my job. I had made my peace with being alone. For one brief, shining moment, when I had seen Dean's name for the interview, I had held out a hope that things might work out. That maybe, despite the years apart, we could be together. Dean had made it painfully clear that he wasn't interested and wanted as little to do with me as possible. Until this phone call, that was.

I picked up the cellphone and dialed his number. It rang four times, and I was about to leave a message to just have a car sent to wherever he was and that the company would pick up the tab, when an unfamiliar voice answered.

"Hello? Who is this?" The voice was gruffer and deeper than Dean's. I glanced at the screen to make sure the number was right.

"This is Rachel Weber. Can you put Dean Sherman on the phone, please?" I asked politely. I wondered where Dean was that someone else would pick up his phone.

"Oh good. He said you'd call. He's here at the bar and is gonna need someone to come get him. He's pretty messed up," the voice said.

"Can I just send a car? Give me the address, and I'll send someone," I replied. I was ready to just go home. Flying with Brandi was exhausting, and my patience was wearing thin.

"No can do, Lady. He says he only wants you, and I'm not tangling with him. He already broke up a bar fight for me, and there is no way in hell I'm going against anything he wants." The guy sounded almost intimidated by Dean. I pinched the ridge of my nose and squeezed my eyes shut. There was no way I was going to make it to the B&B. *Damn you, Dean.*

"All right. Give me the address, and I'll be there as soon as I can. I'm in Tampa right now, so however long that will take," I said, pulling out a pen to write the address on my hand.

"You're about an hour away. Bar's called Revenge. Been here forever," the voice said. I nearly dropped my phone. He didn't need to give me a street address. I knew where that bar was. It was the bar where Dean and I had met.

"Do you need directions?" the voice asked, interrupting the flow of memories.

"Uh, no, I'm good. I'll be there as soon as I can," I stuttered into the phone.

"No problem, lady. I'll try and slow his drinks down so he'll hopefully be ready to sober up," the voice said, and the line clicked off.

I stood in shock for a moment. What was Dean doing at *that* bar? I finally shook myself, trying to clear my head and make my feet move.

I would just go and get him as fast as I could. My phone

said there was an airport close to the bar, so if I could find a plane, I could charter us a flight home. Maybe I could still make the massage I had scheduled for tomorrow if this all went to plan. As soon as I thought those words, though, I knew I had jinxed myself. Things never went "to plan."

CHAPTER 15

June 9th, 1990

THE DAY I was dreading had arrived. Somehow, my week had flown by on silent wings, gliding past on sunshine and happiness. I felt as though I had only just arrived, that I had only just found the starting point. Dean and I were about to begin something wonderful, and it wasn't fair that Dean had to leave. It wasn't fair that we had only had four magical days together, and now he had to leave for the horrors of war. It made my stomach hurt.

I sat on his bed, my arms wrapped around my legs, watching him pack. He had the door to the ocean open, and the salty air was making my hair ripple down my back. Despite the Florida sunshine and the warmth of the breeze, I felt cold.

Dean carefully packed his dark green rucksack, placing his boots and clothing in the hard canvas with care. His slow, methodical movements were hypnotic, the muscles on his arms flexing and relaxing with an attractive rhythm. Maybe if I watched him long enough, his bag would never fill and he would never have to leave.

A knock on his open door drew my attention. There Matt stood, wearing a white t-shirt, jeans, and a frown. "You ready, man?"

"Yeah. I'll be down in a minute." Dean stared at his bag. It had been packed for at least a minute, but he kept rearranging the items as if packing could delay the inevitable. He slid the metal latch through the loops and closed the bag.

The bed creaked softly as he sat beside me. We didn't look at one another; he just took my hand in his, and we sat there for a moment. The ocean sighed behind us, calling like a forgotten lover. The pit in my stomach was growing deeper with every second.

"Are you sure you have to go?" I asked. I had asked it before, and I knew the answer would be the same.

"I told you last night. I have to go back. But I'll be home before you know it." He twisted on the bed so he could face me. With a gentle hand, he brushed a free strand of hair behind my ear and out of my face. His fingers grazed my cheek, his skin rough against the sensitive skin of my jaw. My eyes fluttered up to meet his.

"Promise?" It came out a whisper, my voice betraying me at the last minute. I reached up with my own hand and pressed his to my cheek. I wanted to remember the way his touch felt.

"Promise," he said. He leaned forward and kissed me. I squeezed my eyes shut, memorizing every detail. I wanted to remember his smell, his taste, and the way his lips felt against mine. I would take it with me until he came home.

We broke apart reluctantly, hearing the boys downstairs opening and slamming doors. It was time for them to leave. Dean brushed away a tear I hadn't even realized had escaped and kissed the tip of my nose.

"This won't be for forever. I'll find you." He gave me a confident smile, and I attempted to give him one back. I felt it waver, but I put my heart into it to make it stay. I would see him again. What we had found in this short vacation was too good to let slip through our fingers.

Dean stood, shouldering the heavy bag as though it were weightless. He held out a hand, and I unfolded myself from the bed and took it to steady me as I straightened. I let his hand go for a moment, to smooth the bedspread and close the door. The room became a foreign place as the song of the ocean cut off. We were leaving, and the house was losing its magic.

I took his hand, feeling his strength infuse me as we navigated the stairs down to the main room where the others were waiting. They all looked as miserable as the two of us.

Kimberly and Tony stood off in a corner, their foreheads pressed together, whispering secrets. Matt and Jenny sat on separate couches, deliberately not looking at one another. Jenny held her head high as she stared out a window.

As soon as we arrived, Matt picked up his bag and opened the main door. The two cars sat in the driveway, their windows staring at me like soulless monsters. They were going to take the boys away. The thought of slashing the tires raced through my mind, but I knew it would only be a delay. They would have to leave eventually. We trickled out of the house, moving slowly, hoping time would stop.

The boys' rental car let out a metallic groan as Matt's bag landed with a thud in the trunk. Dean's bag followed close behind it, while Tony's bag went into Jenny's beat-up little car. She had to slam the lid three times before the rusty trunk finally latched. We all stood in the hot sunshine, unsure of how to procrastinate further.

Matt flopped into the driver's seat of his car, Jenny moving slowly to the passenger side. Dean and I wiggled into the backseat, sliding on the pleather interior. It smelled like plastic and gas, but at least I was with him.

Kimberly started Jenny's car, the high pitched whine filling our ears as Tony locked the front door and hid the keys under the doormat. His aunt would pick them up the next day. He gave the house one last lingering look before turning and reluctantly getting into the beat-up station wagon with Kim. The house seemed to stare after us with vacant, sad eyes as we all pulled away and headed for the airport.

We sat quietly in the backseat, gripping one another's hands. I leaned my head on Dean's shoulder, and he kissed my hair. I was glad I couldn't see his face because I knew I would cry and wouldn't be able to stop. I watched the city speed by through the windows, Matt driving exactly the speed limit to the airport. I knew he loved to speed, but he was in no real hurry to get to the airport. He sat stiffly, point-edly ignoring Jenny next to him. She in turn stared out her window as if it were the most interesting thing in the entire world. I might have believed their indifference, if not for the fact that they had their hands clasped together in front of the center console.

CHAPTER 16

June 9th, 1990

THE AIRPORT REARED its ugly gray head all too soon. I swallowed down tears as a plane soared overhead, the jets rumbling through the air. Matt parked the car in the rental station, handing the keys over to a man in a red vest. Matt carried his bag like a suitcase to the check-in line, his big biceps flexed as he moved across the shiny floor.

The moments seemed to blur together, my brain refusing to accept what was going on. I turned to see Tony walking up, his arm draped protectively around Kimberly. She had tears running down her face. The tissue balled in her palm was past its usefulness, but she kept wiping her nose with it anyway.

Dean squeezed my hand, letting me go for a moment, as he checked his bag and picked up his ticket. The three men were ready to head to the gate in less time than I had hoped.

I wanted every moment, every step, to take twice as long as it should because that would be twice as long that I could spend with Dean.

We were at the gate all too soon. Boarding was due to start at any moment; we had almost dallied too long at the house for the boys to make their flight. For a moment I wished we had. Dean pulled me over to a corner with empty chairs. The woman at the airline desk announced that boarding would now begin.

"I wish you didn't have to go," I whispered. He pressed his forehead to mine and wrapped his arms around me. We were in our own world. I looked into his beautiful winter-sky eyes, feeling the tears start to swell behind my eyes. I knew they would escape at any moment.

"I know. It's my duty and I have to. I have your address, though. I'll write you as soon as I get settled." Dean's voice was soft and low with a comforting tone to it. I knew he was as close to breaking as I was, but he was trying to comfort me. "You have my address. It won't be long before we see each other again."

I gave a short nod. My chest was going to explode with the pressure growing in my heart. How did people do this? How did people say goodbye to the ones they loved? How did military husbands and wives do this on a regular basis? I had only known Dean for less than a week, and I was about to lose it. I couldn't imagine the pain of someone with years of love saying goodbye.

I sniffed, the tears threatening to overwhelm me. I didn't want to say goodbye. I would have given anything in that moment for him to stay. We had amazing chemistry, and I wanted to know where we could take it. I wanted to know now, not when he got back.

"I'm giving serious thought to holding onto your ankle

and not letting go, like a little kid. You're going to have to drag me onto the airplane because I'm not letting go," I said. He let out a low chuckle with a sad smile.

"I'm sure the stewardesses will be okay with that. I gave serious thought to just packing you into my duffel bag and taking you with me. I'd rather have you than my boots any day." He touched my cheek, as if to feel me smile. I wanted him to remember me smiling.

"If I'm on your ankle, do you think they'd still give me peanuts?" I asked. Dean snickered and kissed my forehead. The airline attendant was calling out for the last passengers. It was time for Dean to leave.

"I have something for you," Dean said. His voice held such sadness, and the pressure around my chest was intense. I silently begged for the world to stop spinning. "Read it after I'm on the plane."

I nodded weakly. The attendant was calling out again. Dean swallowed hard. He ran his fingers down my hair, the crooked smile I loved crossing his face. He cupped my chin in his fingers and kissed me. I breathed him in. He smelled like soap and sunshine. His mouth was warm and minty. A small patch of beard he missed shaving scratched at my cheek. His hands were strong as he pulled me into him for this one last kiss.

He let me go, his hand caressing my cheek as he stepped back. I kept my eyes closed for a moment, trying to remember every detail. When I opened them, he was walking into the gate. He turned at the last moment, giving me one of his trademarked crooked smiles. He hesitated, as though deciding whether to actually get on the plane or run back into my arms, but he turned and stepped through the door. And then he was gone.

THE CAR RIDE back to our condo was silent. Kimberly sat in the backseat, her head resting against the window as she stared off into space. Her cheeks were dry, but every once in a while she let out a quiet whimper. Jenny drove, her jaw clenched and her knuckles white around the steering wheel. The letter Dean had given me sat in my pocket, but I wanted to be alone to read it.

When we arrived back at our tiny rental, we all disappeared into different corners of the house. Later, we would finish packing and make the long drive home, but for now, we each wanted to be alone. The boys of summer were gone and off to war, and we all knew that they may never come home.

I sat on the edge of my twin bed, the sunlight streaming in around my shoulders. My hair was hot on the back of my neck, so I drew it up into a ponytail and out of my face. I held Dean's letter in my hands, almost afraid to open it. There were a million things, both exhilarating and terrifying, I hoped it could say.

With trembling fingers, I unfolded the paper, smoothing out the creases from the trip in my pocket and began to read:

 Dear Rachel,

I've fallen hard for you. No one has ever made me feel the way you do. I don't think anyone ever will again.

I wish I could put into words how happy I am when I'm with you. I want you to know that I'll think of you often and it will always put a smile on my face.

I'll find you when I come home.
I love you.
Dean

A tear fell onto the paper, turning the white paper translucent. I quickly wiped it off before it could smear the ink, then pressing the paper into my chest. I felt heavy and light at the same time. I wanted to sing and cry and dance and scream all at once.

Dean loved me.

CHAPTER 17

wo Years Ago

I HAD to turn on the GPS guidance on my phone when I got into town. Everything was different, and even though the bar was still in the same spot, the buildings, and even the beach, were not. I finally found it, maneuvering the rental car into the quiet parking lot.

What had once been the hottest disco bar in the small town was now a rundown country bar. Gravel and sand crunched under my feet as I headed up the rickety wooden steps toward the open door. It looked as though they had covered the open air portion of the bar. Bad country music blared out into the parking lot, the dim light from the bar glowing neon yellow and red.

Inside, a girl with full tattoo sleeves leaned against the jukebox, feeding it quarters and singing along with the music. I could see where a fight had occurred earlier, a chair in pieces by the door. Several males were in a smoky corner, taking turns around a faded green pool table, but I wasn't there for them. I was there for the long-legged man sitting hunched at the bar, surrounded by empty whiskey glasses.

The bartender stood behind the bar, wiping a glass clean with a dirty towel. He saw me walk in, his eyes going up and down, and then again. He nodded toward Dean, setting the clean glass in a rack by the sink. I walked confidently to the tall bar.

"Dean, what are you doing?" I asked. Dean turned, his eyes languid but unsurprised.

"Getting drunk off my ass. Care to join me?"

"No. I want to get you to a hotel and me on a plane. It's time for us to go," I said. I grabbed his arm, feeling the strong muscle tense underneath my fingers. He pulled away from me, shaking his head.

"Leave me alone. It's what you're good at." He turned back to the bar, motioning for another whiskey. The bartender pretended not to see him.

His words stung. We had been politely distant since his hire, but that was as much his fault as mine. I wondered if he had been as lonely as I had. I sighed. We needed to fix this if we were going to work together. Our stony silence was not conducive to a working relationship, and with Jack transitioning to power in the next few weeks, Dean and I were going to be put together more and more often.

"Two whiskeys, neat." I motioned to the bartender. He quickly poured two whiskeys into glasses, sliding them directly to me. I picked them both up, stepping back and heading toward a small booth against the wall. I stopped and held one out to Dean. "Come sit with me. Like old times."

He looked at me warily, but then stood. Even while inebriated he moved with a deadly grace. He sat in the cheap plastic booth, taking the whiskey glass from me and nursing it gently. His eyes, those oceans of blue, watched me carefully. I took the whiskey in one swig.

"Will you tell me what you are doing here? This is a little out of the way to stop for a drink on the way home." I glanced around the bar. Our relationship was like this bar: once beautiful but now rundown and empty.

Dean sipped at his drink and cautiously eyed me. "Reliving old wounds."

I bit the inside of my cheek. I didn't want to be vain, but I had a feeling he was at least partially referencing me. "You want to talk about it?"

"What? Are we friends now?" Dean sneered and finished his drink. He motioned to the bartender for another and I nodded approval.

"Listen, Dean, I know we have some issues. I'd like to change that. Can we just pretend we never met each other until your interview? Water under the bridge and all that. Start from scratch." I watched him carefully. His face twitched for a moment, and then he leaned back in the booth, crossing his arms.

"Fine. We start over," he said. The bartender set two fresh glasses on the table. I waited for Dean to reach for his before I picked mine up. He sipped on his drink, and then, changing his mind, downed the rest of it in one go. I drank mine slowly, feeling the liquid burn down my throat and my body relax. I had needed a drink after today.

"It's all different now," Dean said. His voice was quiet, barely carrying over the noise of the jukebox. He stared at the empty glass in his hands, twirling it and letting it catch the dim bar light. "I went by Frontera's place. It isn't there anymore. It's a huge hotel now."

I sipped at my drink. Dean stared at his empty glass as

though he could will it to fill, but he made no attempt to refill it.

"What are you doing here, Dean?" I asked again. He set the glass carefully on the table.

"It was my fault." His eyes never left the glass, lost in his own world. I sat quietly, wondering what exactly he meant. "It was my fault Frontera died."

The admission was kind of a shock to me, but he couldn't have been responsible. "What do you mean, it was your fault?"

He looked up at me, his blue eyes cold. "I had to choose between the mission and my friend. I chose the mission."

I swirled the last few drops in my glass. Dean looked up at me, as though asking forgiveness.

"We were supposed to guard a Kuwaiti VIP. Shit went down. I had to decide between protecting the VIP and completing the mission or saving Frontera... I completed the mission." Dean's voice cracked, and he took the glass from my hand and finished my drink. I let him.

I now understood why he was here, in this bar and drinking like a fish. Today he had to choose between his client and someone else. He chose the client. This time it had cost him nothing, but last time it had cost him his friend. This bar was where he and Frontera had been happiest before Frontera's death. That it happened to be a place significant to me as well was just an unlucky item of misery to add to his guilt.

I got out of my seat and slid into his. He didn't fight as I wrapped my arms around his shoulders, pulling him to me. His body shook with silent sobs. It was twenty years, but he hadn't forgiven himself yet.

I remembered Tony's shy smile. I remembered the way

he and Kimberly whispered in the corners, wrapped up in a serendipitous love. It broke my heart.

Dean quieted, his body no longer shaking. "I was shot during that mission. So was Grinswald. I told them it hurt to hold a rifle because of the wound, and they let me out. Truth was, I couldn't stand to be in the military anymore. I lost one of my best friends, and another one nearly died for nothing."

We sat there, silent. He was broken in a way that I would never understand, a way I never wanted to understand, but I didn't want him to be alone.

He glanced over at me, and I recognized the look well. Those eyes were undressing me, and I couldn't say that I didn't like it. "You know, I kinda want to check out that hotel where Frontera's place used to be. Do you want to come with me?"

I knew exactly what we'd be doing if we went to check out that hotel, and even with just the couple of drinks that I had, I was sorely tempted. I looked down at his muscular arms, wondering how well he had kept in shape...

I shook my head. "No, Dean. There's a flight that leaves the airport near here in an hour. We should be on that flight."

He turned to face me. "Come on, I just want to have a peek."

A peek at the rooms, or a peek at me? "Dean, I'll close out your tab, and we can go."

He sighed, then staggered over to the bar. I blew out a whole lungful of air. It had been close, but I had resisted. I knew that if we did something, we would both regret it in the morning and we both had enough regrets to last a lifetime. We didn't need any more.

I walked Dean out to the car. On the way to the airport,

we passed the spot where the old surf shop had been. It was a Sunglasses Hut now. Dean groaned loudly.

"Everything's changed, hasn't it?" he asked, sounding heartbroken through his drunken slur.

"Yes, it has," I said.

"This town will never be the same, will it? We'll never be the same, will we?" I heard a drunken sob leave his body.

I put my hand on his shoulder. I wanted to comfort him, but I had to keep my distance. "Maybe it's for the best." He didn't have an answer to that, but I felt him sob a few more times.

Dean managed to act sober long enough for us to get on the plane. Before the plane even took off, his head was on my shoulder. He was snoring softly, just as he had been when I first woke up next to him. I felt like sobbing myself.

CHAPTER 18

*J*une 16*th*, *1990*

I STUMBLED INTO MY APARTMENT, dropping the stack of bills on my kitchen table. They merged seamlessly with the other bills and junk mail, all waiting for me to be responsible and look at them. Nothing I was hoping for had come in the mail. I closed the door and kicked off my shoes, letting my toes stretch out and relax. I had been home for a week and was missing the beach terribly. No, I didn't miss the beach. I missed Dean. Six days, eight hours, and thirty-seven minutes since I had seen him last. And I had no idea how to fill the hole that was growing in my heart.

I leaned back against the door, closing my eyes and remembering his face. Maybe a letter would come tomorrow. I had sent one off two days ago, carefully checking and then double-checking the address. It had been hard to write, not knowing where to start and then not knowing where to curb my words. I wanted to tell him that he was all I could think about, that I would wait for him to come back if he wanted. But I had no idea how to put that in a letter without sounding overenthusiastic or sappy. What if he didn't feel the same way? What if he had just been using me to have a good time before he disappeared back to war? For all I knew, he actually had a boring sales job and the whole going off to Saudi Arabia was just a really good cover story.

No, I told myself, *he really was into me*. There was no way he could have faked all of it. No one was that good. Besides, he didn't have to give me the letter; he only would have done that if our time together had meant something to him too. I wasn't sure if that made my heart ache more or less. I wished for the umpteenth time that he was here and not far away. I completely ignored the fact that he was probably in mortal danger at that moment because that was just one straw too many. I knew I would break if I tried to carry that knowledge too.

I jumped as a knock sounded on the door behind me. The peephole showed a well-dressed man in a business suit, the sun shining warmly around him. I opened the door, cautiously peeking around the heavy wood to see what he wanted.

"Ms. Weber? Ms. Rachel Weber?" the man asked in a thin, nasal voice. His suit was nicer than I had expected. It was definitely a designer label from this year. Maybe he was one of the designers I had applied for an internship with!

"That's me. How can I help you?" I hoped I didn't sound too eager. His shoes were also from this season.

"My name is Edward Martinez. I'm a representative for someone who is very interested in your design work." He pushed a pair of oversized glasses back up higher on his nose.

"My design work? That's wonderful! Please, come in," I said, opening the door. He stepped inside, glancing at the stack of mail on my table before discretely looking away. He was probably in his early forties; his hair was still dark but the creases around his brown eyes gave him away. He settled gracefully on the couch as I hurried to close the door and join him.

"Ms. Weber, my employer would like to ask you to come out to New York for a consultation. She was very impressed by your work and would like to meet you." Mr. Martinez gave me a warm smile, and I couldn't help but to return it.

"That sounds wonderful. Who is your employer?" I suddenly had a horrible, sinking feeling that this was all a scam. I imagined him telling me that for the low, low price of just $99.99, he would be happy to introduce me to someone in the industry.

Mr. Martinez pulled a card from the inside of his suit pocket and handed it to me. In beautiful swirly, gold letters the name Bianca Saunders dominated the card. I didn't recognize the name, and there was nothing else on the card to give me any hints as to who she might be. Bianca Saunders was not one of the major fashion houses I had applied to.

"I'm afraid I don't know who this is," I said slowly. Mr. Martinez's face fell a little.

"You don't know who Bianca Saunders is?" Mr. Martinez frowned and looked at me like I might be an alien.

"No, I don't." I handed him back the card, but he just held up his hand for me to keep it.

"Bianca Saunders is the wife of Daniel Saunders..." he said slowly, waiting for me to recognize the name. When my face stayed blank, he continued, "...of DS Oil and Gas. You know, the huge billion-dollar oil company? One of the only oil companies that's not being affected by the current events in Kuwait?"

Just the mention of Kuwait made me think of Dean. Was that where he was now? I shook my head at Mr. Martinez slowly. Despite everything he said, I had never even heard of the company.

"Well, Mrs. Saunders saw your senior design project, and she is incredibly interested in meeting you. She is hoping you can design more like it." Mr. Martinez crossed his legs and settled into the couch.

"She liked my design? That's fantastic!" I felt elation run through me. My professors had loved that I had created something fashionable for a pregnant woman to wear. I knew it was an under-served market, and that it was probably a poor choice for a senior project, but I had made something similar for my aunt, and when the project came due, the fabric had taken a life of its own. Other than my professors, though, no one had expressed any interest in my design.

"Yes. As such, she has arranged for you to come out to New York City. She would like to see more of your designs and meet you in person." He leaned in conspiratorially. "If she likes what she sees, she is interested in hiring you for your entire fall line."

I sat back in my chair, trying to keep myself from getting over-excited. My design was for a pregnant woman, so if Mrs. Saunders was interested in it, that must have meant she was pregnant. She was also a very wealthy lady. If I designed the clothing for her pregnancy, and she wore it to social events, I would become a household name. Even though it would be for maternity wear, this was an opportunity I couldn't resist.

"Well, Mr. Martinez, I am definitely interested, but I'm

afraid I don't really have the financial means to be traveling to New York City without some sort of assistance." These were fancy words meaning that I was poor.

Mr. Martinez smiled, his teeth gleaming a perfect shade of white. "Of course. Mrs. Saunders has already arranged for the flight, your room and board, and a small assessment fee. She understands that you are a busy woman, and that she must pay for your time." He took an envelope out of his pocket, making me wonder just what else he had stashed in his jacket, and handed it to me.

Inside there was a check for a thousand dollars. I swallowed hard. It had my name on it.

"That is for agreeing to meet with her. She is willing to pay double that for the original garment to be made to her specifications. As it is a custom fitting, she would like you to be there to do it," Mr. Martinez said. "If everything is satisfactory, she will consign more garments."

The check shook slightly in my hands, as though I were experiencing a small earthquake. "You said she's taken care of all the travel expenses?"

Mr. Martinez nodded. He had a slight smile, as though he were secretly amused by my reactions. "The flight is scheduled for tomorrow morning."

I looked up. This was too good an opportunity to miss. If nothing else, the fee for making her the dress would pay my rent for a while. If things went as well as my imagination was starting to think it could, I wouldn't need to worry about rent anymore.

"Well, Mr. Martinez, what kind of weather should I pack for?"

CHAPTER 19

*J*une 20th, 1990

I GRIPPED MY SKETCHBOOK TIGHTLY, making sure for the third time that I still had the designs from the night before. I had no idea what Mrs. Saunders looked like, how far along in her pregnancy she was, or what her build might be. I had sketched out a couple more maternity designs, but without meeting her, I didn't want to create too many, but I needed enough to impress.

Mr. Martinez walked calmly in front of me, easily navigating the huge apartment building as we headed toward what he called "Mrs. Saunders' sun-room". The apartment was huge; bigger than what I would consider a house. I had a feeling the oil business, at least for the Saunders and DS Oil and Gas, was doing well.

I was trying my very best not to be overwhelmed by everything, and I felt like I was doing a pretty good job. Mr.

Martinez and I had arrived by a private plane and then drove straight into the city to the Saunders' household. I couldn't wait to go out and explore the city after my interview. The buildings had called out to me, the streets singing that I was in the right place. I had been here less than an hour, and I already loved New York.

Mr. Martinez knocked politely on a beautiful wooden door. A female voice called for us to come in, and Mr. Martinez opened the heavy door. I followed his steps, trying to exude as much confidence as I could muster. At least I felt dressed for the occasion. I was wearing my most recent design for myself: slate gray dress pants with a matching vest over a dress shirt. It was based off of a traditional men's suit, but fit to flare out and highlight femininity. It seemed appropriate attire for meeting with a powerful woman.

A petite blonde woman stood gracefully. She was just starting her pregnancy, a gentle curve beginning to grace her middle. I smiled inwardly; I knew my senior project would look amazing on her tiny frame.

"Mrs. Saunders, let me introduce Rachel Weber," Mr. Martinez presented me as I walked into the room. I held out my hand, making eye contact with my future employer.

"It's a pleasure to meet you," I said politely. Mrs. Saunders shook my hand with a strength that surprised me. Her brown eyes looked me up and down, measuring and weighing me better than any tailor I had ever met. There was a steel in her look that impressed me. It was clear this woman always got what she wanted.

"Ms. Weber, it's a pleasure to meet you in person. Thank you, Edward, that will be all." The blonde woman never took her eyes off of me as she dismissed Mr. Martinez. I heard him close the door quietly behind him as he left.

"Please, sit down, Ms. Weber. Tell me about yourself. What inspired you to design this piece?"

Mrs. Saunders sat on an upholstered loveseat, offering me a position in a matching chair. I sat carefully, mindful of my posture. It seemed like posture would matter to this woman. The room was decorated with a feminine, yet incredibly practical, theme.

I took a deep breath and began talking. "Well, I just graduated with my degree in fashion and design..."

"I don't need your resume, I already have that," she cut me off. I swallowed and took a moment to evaluate my situation and try again to present my best self. I glanced around the room, taking it in and forming her personality in my mind based off of the design. The uncomfortable upholstered furniture told me that appearances mattered to this woman. She wore a designer sweater and dress pants, but the seams were struggling to support her growing middle. *She wants to keep up appearances.* Her ring was a simple diamond solitaire that couldn't have cost more than a couple hundred dollars. *She hadn't always been rich, but the ring must be sentimental. She loves her husband,* I thought. Several photos on the wall caught my attention; they were of a small boy playing with a smiling man I assumed was her husband. She was pregnant with her second child, then.

"My dad died when I was little, and my mom died when I was in high school," I started. "My aunt finished raising me, but she was more of a friend than a guardian since she was only a few years older than I was. Last summer, she got pregnant with her first child. She hated maternity clothes. She has a figure very similar to yours, and everything was incredibly baggy and loose. Ugly floral patterns, awful stretchy denim with no pockets, and jumpers designed to fit a whale. It was terrible." I paused for a moment, catching my breath.

"Go on," she said, a slight smile pulling on her lips. If she was looking for maternity wear, she knew the fashion horrors I was referencing.

"She had a big party for her husband's job," I continued. "She was ready to pretend to be sick so she didn't have to wear the only dress she could find that would fit, despite it making her look like a giant balloon. I love my aunt. So, as a surprise, I made her a dress."

I smiled at the memory of my aunt's amazed expression and the tears of joy that had streamed down her face when I showed her the dress I made her. She had hugged me like I was the biggest hero in the world. The next day she had come over to my house with brownies, raving about how everyone couldn't stop complimenting her dress. She said she felt beautiful for the first time in months.

"It was just a simple black dress, but I designed it to bring out what was beautiful about her. Even though she was pregnant, she didn't have to feel huge and out of place. She loved it. It became the basis for my senior design piece." I couldn't decide what to do with my hands as I finished, so I simply folded them on the top of my design notebook and waited for Mrs. Saunders' response.

"So, your senior design is what your aunt wore?" Mrs. Saunders frowned slightly, as though I were trying to pass off something used as new.

"Oh no, I didn't mean to imply that," I said quickly. "The design for my aunt was simply the starting point. I didn't even mean for the idea to go anywhere, but once I started brainstorming things for her, I couldn't stop. The design I submitted for my senior project has never been worn. My aunt gave me feedback about what she liked and disliked about the dress, and then I added my own twist."

I held up the dress and pointed to parts of it. "The fabric, the collar, the sleeves, the length, and the back are all different. If you held the two dresses up, the only real similarity is that they are both designed for a pregnant woman," I said. Mrs. Saunders clearly wanted something unique, and I chewed nervously on the inside of my lip. I didn't want to screw this up.

"I see." Mrs. Saunders nodded, her face revealing nothing. Sweat trickled down my spine. I couldn't afford to miss out on this opportunity. "Do you have more designs like it, or is it the only one of its kind?"

I grinned and opened my sketchbook. This is where I knew I would shine. I crossed the small space between us and knelt on the floor before her, flipping to my newest designs. She raised a perfectly manicured eyebrow at me as I began pointing out the designs. My excitement surprised her.

"I have several designs here for different stages of a pregnancy. This one is more for the beginning stages, just when things are starting to fit differently, and then this one," I turned the page and pointed to a drawing of a very pregnant woman in a flowing dress, "this one is for the last couple of weeks."

"May I?" Mrs. Saunders asked, reaching for the sketchbook. I nodded and handed it up to her.

"These are just some initial drawings. I would love to make some that are personalized to you and your tastes." I held my breath as she leafed through the drawings. A soft smile started to form on her face. She looked over, her brown eyes warming as the smile took hold.

"I would love to see more. I especially like this one," she

said pointing to a flowing gown in emerald green. "But, I will need business appropriate attire as well."

"I actually have some ideas. Here." I flipped several pages to a series of woman's business suits. They weren't originally designed for maternity, so I hadn't showed them to her yet. "If I modify the seams here, it would look fantastic throughout a pregnancy."

"What about this one?" she asked, pointing to a smart-looking skirt and tight blouse. I frowned slightly.

"I'm not sure I can make that one work once you hit the second trimester. I can make anything fit, but with the cut and shape of the skirt, it would look like I stuffed you into it. If you want it, I'll make it, but I don't think you'll be pleased with the outcome," I answered honestly. Her smile grew a little bit bigger.

"Thank you for being honest. I had to fire my last designer because she said everything looked good, even when it didn't. I need to look professional, not tacky. I help my husband run this business, and I can't let this pregnancy slow me down." She sighed and looked over at the pictures of the little boy on her wall. "When I had Jack, I didn't care what I wore. I was just so excited to be having a child. I look back at those pictures and wonder how anyone took me seriously. With the current market the way it is, I don't have that luxury this time."

A knock on the door interrupted whatever she was going to say next. Mr. Martinez poked his head in. "Mrs. Saunders, your three-o'clock is here," he said softly. Mrs. Saunders nodded and he closed the door carefully behind him.

"Well, Ms. Weber, I think that this will work out wonderfully. I'll have Edward set up an appointment for the two of us so we can get measurements and go over my preferences as well as payment." Mrs. Saunders stood up slowly, and I followed her example.

"I'll make up some more design ideas. It was a pleasure meeting you, Mrs. Saunders, and I look forward to seeing you again." I shook her hand and she smiled warmly.

"Likewise," she said as she walked me to the door. I thanked her again and stepped out into the hallway, letting out a huge sigh of relief once the door closed.

She liked my designs. She wanted me to design more for her. A giddy rush of happiness consumed me and it took all my will power not to dance and sing as Mr. Martinez led me back out to the street and into a waiting car. I was in New York City, and I was going to be designing clothing! This was more than I could have hoped for.

CHAPTER 20

June 20ᵗʰ, 1990

DOWN AT STREET LEVEL, I got into the waiting car and stared out the window. The driver was silent as I headed back to my hotel, and my mind was on designs rather than the giant buildings when something caught my eye. A young boy, about five or six years old, was walking resolutely along the sidewalk. He stopped, setting down a brightly-wrapped present, and pulled out an oversized map, his small face frowning as he tried to read it. The boy obviously was trying to get somewhere to deliver the gift, but I couldn't see an adult with him. I watched him for a moment as we sat at a light, wondering why he looked vaguely familiar.

I gasped as it hit me where I had seen the boy before. He was the laughing child in the pictures on Mrs. Saunders' wall. His mother would be worried sick if she knew he was out on the streets of New York by himself.

"Stop the car!" I shouted, unbuckling my seat-belt and practically lunging for the door. The driver looked back at me in surprise, but quickly pulled to the side of the road. Luckily, the street wasn't very busy, and he was able to find a spot.

"Are you Jack Saunders?" I asked, hurrying over to the blonde-headed boy. He looked up from the map, determination and just a little bit of fear in his big eyes. He nodded.

"Who are you?" he asked. His little voice didn't tremble, but he puffed out his chest and stood taller, trying to be bigger than he was. The warm wind ruffled his blonde hair, giving him a defiant look.

"My name's Rachel. Your mom just hired me to make her some clothes," I answered honestly. "Are you lost?"

"You're the lady who made the dress she likes?" he asked, looking up at me. His small mouth was pinching up on one side as he evaluated me. He must have decided I was trustworthy because he pointed to his map and said, "I'm trying to get to my dad's office."

"Okay. Can I help you?" I asked, crouching down to be on his level. His big eyes somehow got even bigger as he nodded. He was doing a good job of not being afraid, but he knew he had bitten off more than he could chew. He handed me the map, his eyes watching me cautiously to make sure I didn't run off with it.

I took the map from his small hands, turning it right side up, and looked at it carefully. Circled in red crayon was an intersection where I assumed was his father's office building was located. He pointed at the circle and looked over at me.

"That's Daddy's office. I have a present for him. Yesterday was Father's Day, but he was busy at work, so I didn't get to give him my present. Mommy said I could go see him today, but then she got busy, so I am doing it myself." He gave me a toothy grin. "Daddy's going to love my present. I worked really hard on it."

I grinned right back at him and folded up the map. "How about we let my driver take us? This looks like a pretty long walk from here."

He looked over at the car, picked up his present, and hurried over to the passenger door. I made a mental note to mention to Mrs. Saunders how easily I had convinced him to come with me. Five minutes was all it took and I loved the kid already. I found myself grinning as I walked toward the car, the little boy's excitement infectious.

He slid into the back seat and waved to the driver. "Ms. Rachel says you can drive me to my dad's office," Jack told him. The driver looked over at me as I crawled in beside the little boy. I nodded and handed the driver the map. He turned it in his hands, his eyebrows raising at the crayon circle, but he started the engine and pulled out into the street. I was glad he knew where we were going, because I had no idea.

Jack fastened his seat-belt and carefully placed the present in his lap before reminding me that I should be wearing a seat-belt too. I quickly clicked the belt into place, and he gave me another toothy grin.

"What did you get your dad?" I asked, nodding toward the box in his lap.

"I didn't get him anything. I made it." Pride beamed off his small features. He held up the box for me to look at. "I even wrapped it myself."

"I think homemade gifts are even better than ones you buy. What did you *make* him?" I asked, making sure to emphasize the corrected word.

"I made him a picture frame. Mommy helped me get the

picture- it's of Daddy and me playing football, but I deco-rated the frame all by myself. I also made him a card. See?" The little boy held up an envelope with the word "Daddy" scrawled in messy handwriting.

"I am sure your dad is going to love it." I patted his knee gently and he beamed up at me. He pointed to the card and started telling me all about the colors and stickers he used. I let him babble on, nodding appropriately and asking simple questions. The more I sat and listened to him, the happier he became. It made me wonder just how much time he got with adults actually paying attention to him.

The car rolled to a stop in front of a tall gray building. The summer light reflected off the windows as we stepped out onto the sidewalk. I told the driver I was going to make sure Jack got to his father's office safely.

"I'll just park in the employee lot over there. When ever you are ready, just come get me. Take your time- I'm at your disposal for the rest of the afternoon," he told me. I felt my city exploring time fading away, but Jack's excitement at getting to see his father more than made up for it.

As we walked into the lobby, a security guard recognized Jack and made his way over. Jack beamed up at the big man, waving and showing him the present.

"Hey, little man, is that for your dad?" the guard asked. When Jack nodded furiously, the guard laughed. "How about I take you two up there to see him, then?"

We followed behind the guard, Jack chattering up a storm as we stepped into an elevator. He didn't stop the flow of words the entire way up. The guard lead us to a large desk with a busy secretary.

"I'd like to see my father, please," the little boy chirped up at her. She leaned over the desk and gave him a warm smile. It was apparent the boy was a common sight around the office, as workers often stopped to smile and wave.

"Hi, Jack! Your dad's in a meeting right now, but I can let you see him as soon as he's done. It'll be about fifteen minutes." She looked up at me. "Are you two okay waiting that long?"

I nodded. *They must all think I'm taking care of him*, I thought. She reached under her desk, pulling out a stack of coloring books with crayons. Jack carefully took them and carried them to a couch with a small table. He carefully set his gift down, then spread out the crayons, organizing them by color before opening one of the coloring books.

"May I color too?" I asked, settling myself on the floor next to him.

Jack nodded and handed me a book. "You can have this one. I don't like it."

I glanced down at the book. It was full of numbers, all drawn to look like cartoon characters with big eyes and funny gloved hands. Inside the numbers were doing math problems.

"Why don't you like it?" I asked. I had a sneaking suspicion it was because math was involved.

"Because math is dumb," Jack said, looking up at me, his eyes full of what he thought to be knowledge. "I'm never gonna need that."

I managed to keep a straight face as a future business owner told me he didn't need math. Math like addition and subtraction. He was going to have a heck of a time with payroll when he got older.

"That's too bad. I have a cool magic trick, but you have to be able to do math for me to be able to show it to you," I said, picking up a crayon. I started to color the number four a nice shade of purple.

"A magic trick?" Jack asked. He stopped coloring, obviously interested.

"Yeah. I can tell the future. But, it involves math, so you probably wouldn't like it," I said, switching my purple crayon for a blue one.

"But I like magic tricks," he said, a pout crossing his face. I knew I had him. No kid can resist a magic trick. "I wanna see your magic trick."

"Well, I *guess* I can show you," I replied, making sure to exaggerate my shrug. I heard the secretary snicker at her desk, a knowing smile on her face.

"Yeah! Show me! Please!" Jack came around so he could sit closer to me. I found a blank page in one of the coloring books, and ripped off a corner before handing it to Jack.

I leaned in and starting explaining the directions carefully. "Okay. I want you to think of a three digit number that's digits are decreasing. It can be any number you want, but it can't be the same written forward or backward. So, 432 will work, but 121 or 456 won't. That make sense?" I handed Jack a crayon and he nodded.

"I am going to write down what your number is going to be in the future." I wrote down '1089' on my ripped corner, then turned it upside-down on the table in front of Jack. "That is going to be your number. Now you write the number you have in your head down on this piece of paper."

"Can you see the number?" He asked, carefully hiding his number with his hand.

"Yes. Since I already wrote down what your future number will be, I can see it." Jack had chosen 431. "Now, subtract the mirror of this number. So subtract 134."

Jack carefully wrote out the numbers and began working his way through the problem. I helped him cross out the numbers and borrow from the bigger column. It took a moment but we got to the correct answer of 297.

"Is that the number you guessed?" Jack asked excitedly.

"We aren't done yet. We did subtraction, now we need some addition. We now need to add the mirror of this number." I watched as he furrowed his brow in concentration and looked at the numbers.

He carefully wrote 792 with a plus sign.

"Perfect. Now add them together, and I will show you that I knew the future," I whispered dramatically. Jack went to work, using his fingers to help him add, and without any help from me, he proudly displayed the number 1089.

I flipped the ripped piece of paper over, revealing the magic 1089 number I had written to begin with, and Jack clapped his hands in delight. "How'd you do that? You really must be magic!"

"It's just math. Still think it's stupid?" I asked.

He gave me a thoughtful look. "Maybe not all math is stupid. Could you show me another one?"

I laughed. "How about I show you how I did that one?"

He nodded furiously and I was about to get another piece of paper when the door behind the secretary's desk opened and two businessmen walked out. A handsome third man followed, his features strongly resembling Jack's.

"Daddy!" the young boy cried out, the magic math problem forgotten as his father welcomed him into a hug.

"What are you doing here, young man?" The older Saunders gave his son a warm smile. The stress sluiced off of his shoulders as he held his young son.

"I came to bring you a present. I got lost, but Ms. Rachel helped me," Jack said, pointing back to where I still sat surrounded by crayons.

"Well, that was very nice of her," Mr. Saunders said. He walked over to shake my hand. "I don't believe we've met."

"We haven't, sir. I'm Rachel Weber. I saw him walking along the street by himself, and I thought he could use some help," I said, feeling suddenly self-conscious.

"Rachel Weber? The designer my wife won't stop talking about?" Daniel Saunders' blue eyes caught mine, showing me a depth of warmth and intelligence.

"I guess that's me," I said, feeling a blush starting in my cheeks.

"Daddy, Daddy! Ms. Rachel showed me a math trick! She says she'll teach it to me!" Jack interjected, pulling on his father's clothing. Mr. Saunders laughed and ruffled his hair.

"Did she, now? My Jack excited about a math trick? You must have supernatural powers, Ms. Rachel," he said with a wink. "Grab that present I see there and the two of you come into my office."

Jack scrambled for the present, a never-ending flow of words pouring from his mouth as he started to tell his father about how he sneaked out from the house and found his way here. I was given a hero's treatment in his story. Daniel nodded, and once we were all in his office, he pulled the young boy onto his lap, laughing as Jack handed him the present.

"Open it, open it!" Jack squealed. Daniel opened the wrapper carefully, letting the suspense build until Jack was nearly vibrating with excitement.

"Oh, Jack! This is beautiful! I'll put it right here on my desk where everyone can see it. Thank you, Son." Daniel said. He gave Jack a big hug, and Jack beamed with pride.

"Oh, I forgot the card. It's out on the table. I'll go get it," Jack said. He jumped from his father's lap and hurried out the door.

As soon as Jack was out the door, Daniel turned to me. "Thank you for taking care of him. He sneaks out to try and see me whenever he can. You didn't have to stop and pick him up, and I really appreciate it," Daniel said. His blue eyes caught mine again. They were darker than Dean's, with almost a green coloring. My heart hurt a little bit just thinking about him. I wondered if I would ever see blue eyes again without thinking of Dean's.

"He's a good kid. He was so excited to bring you your Father's Day gift." I smiled as I looked out the door. Jack had gotten distracted and was showing the secretary his hand-made card. She was oohing and ahhing appropriately and that was making Jack's face light up.

"I can't thank you enough. That boy is the light of my world. I am making this company all that it can be so he can take it over someday." Daniel's gaze followed my own, a smile of pride at his son caressing his features.

"Maybe he and his sibling will run it together," I mused.

"What?" he asked, as if he didn't realize he had another kid on the way. "Oh, perhaps. To be honest, we weren't expecting this second one. Well, if the little one takes an interest in business, then he, or she, is more than welcome to help Jack run it. I just want them to be happy and for the business to stay in the family." Daniel sat down behind his desk and picked up the photograph, the messy stickers and paint of the frame making him smile. He made sure to place it where it would be prominently displayed.

Jack ran into the office, his cheeks pink with smiles as he handed the card to his father. Daniel read it out loud and set it in a place of honor next to the picture frame.

"What did you do for your dad for Father's Day, Ms. Rachel?" Jack asked, turning to face me. "If you forgot, you could use our phone to call him."

"That's very kind of you, Jack, but I can't call him. My dad died when I was little, so I can't call him on the phone. Thank you, though," I answered. Jack and Daniel both looked at me with sad eyes. There was definitely more of Daniel than Bianca in Jack.

"You can share my dad with me then." A big smile spread across Jack's face as he came up with the idea. "He's a pretty good dad, and then you can stay with me in my fort."

"Thank you, Jack. That is very kind of you. You must be a good sharer." I said, managing to keep a straight face. Daniel was beet red, shaking his head at his son. "I should head back to my hotel. I need to get some designs down on paper to show Mrs. Saunders tomorrow."

"Do you have to go?" Jack whined. "I wanted to learn how to do that math trick."

"Still interested in that math trick, huh?" Daniel looked down at his son.

"Ms. Rachel promised to show me how she did it. I did the addition part all by myself! I like math now!" Jack bounced up and down on the balls of his feet.

Daniel leaned over and put his hands on Jack's shoulders, a serious look on his face. "Who are you, and what have you done with my son?" Jack giggled.

"I'll show you how to do it another time. Until then, just practice that subtraction. You were so close to doing it all on your own," I said, kneeling down to his level. He grinned at me and gave me a hug. It surprised me, but I hugged him back.

Daniel watched us for a moment, a smile starting to form as an idea took hold. "Ms. Rachel, what are your current job plans, other than designing some clothing for my wife?"

I sighed. "Well, I'm waiting to hear back on some internships, but given that it's June, I'm not holding my breath." I stood up from hugging Jack, smoothing the fabric on my vest.

Daniel's smile continued to grow. "Would you possibly be interested in a job? I think I have something that would be perfect for you."

CHAPTER 21

*resent Day*

THE DRIVE WAS JUST AS AWKWARD as I was afraid it was going to be. I drove carefully, heading down the highway to the small town on the Atlantic coast. The county jail was only a couple of blocks from the marina. I had, unfortunately, been there to pick Robbie up for public intoxication. Twice. The hospital was only a few streets down from that; luckily, I had never been there, but it would be easy enough to find.

Dean sat comfortably in the passenger seat, his long legs crossed as he looked out the window. We had started out making polite conversation, remarking on the weather- it was supposed to rain later- and how the football season was going. Neither one of us really had the time to follow sports, so that was a short conversation. I didn't really want to discuss the current situation with Dean, and anything regarding the Saunders family was dangerous due to Daniel's condition. Our usually easy conversations, just didn't seem to flow. Our minds were elsewhere. As a result, we sat in silence, listening to the radio. At least we both liked the oldies radio station.

About halfway there, the sky started to drip. At first it was just a couple of big, wet drops, splattering across the windshield. Our little black car hurtled forward, undaunted, into the darkening clouds. Lightning flashed, blinding the sky. I glanced over at Dean as the thunder shook the car windows.

"Some storm, huh?" I gave him a nervous smile.

He nodded, uncrossing his legs and leaning forward in his seat to peer out the windshield at the threatening sky. As if just looking had torn a hole in the sky, rain began to pour. Water sloshed across the road, the falling rain too thick to see through. I tapped on the brakes, feeling the car wiggle on the wet road. Lightning seared across the sky, thunder hot on its heels. This was not a good place to be.

I zeroed in on the brake-lights of the car in front of me, barely able to see them through the storm. Without warning, the car lurched, water stealing the wheels and veering us off the road. I made an undignified sound as I managed to keep control of the car, keeping it from flipping as we hydroplaned across the highway. Lightning scorched the sky, blinding me as I struggled to keep the car from sending the two of us to a watery grave.

I barely registered the thunder, the smearing rain on the windows, or the strange sound the tires made as they powered through the river running down the road. From the corner of my eye, I could see Dean bracing himself against the car, a frown pulling his eyebrows together.

Our last kiss was all I could think of. The way his lips felt soft against mine. The little patch of skin he had missed while shaving that tickled my cheek. His hands, the way the pressed me into him, the way his body held mine like we were made for one another. Imminent death made me think of losing him like I did so many years ago. The steering wheel lurched as we came out of the hydroplane and onto solid pavement again, sucking me out of my memory. I pulled off on the closest shoulder, my knuckles white around the steering wheel.

"You okay?" Dean asked, putting a hand on my arm. I gave him a weak smile, still gripping the steering wheel like the car might fly off at any second. He gave me one of his perfect crooked grins, put on the parking break, and slid his hand down my arm. His skin was warm against mine, his hand infusing a calm energy into me. He carefully unpried my fingers from the steering wheel, wrapping his hand around mine. I realized I was shaking.

"Are *you* okay?" I asked. I held onto his hand, afraid he might take it away. My heart was pounding in my ears, the adrenaline of almost crashing giving me a jittery high. His hand was the only thing keeping me grounded.

"A little rain can't faze me," he answered. "You did a nice job back there."

"Thanks. That was intense!" I gave a short laugh. A tendril of hair had escaped my bun again, and with my free hand, I pushed it behind my ear. "I think we'll just wait this out for a little bit. Robbie won't appreciate it if we never arrive because we're dead."

Dean nodded and peered up through the windshield again. Seeing only the pounding rain, he unbuckled his seat-belt and settled into the chair. He kept my hand clasped firmly in his, as though he were afraid *I* would let go. Thunder rattled the glass, the storm raging around us. Rain pelted the car with angry drops, creating a metallic music on the roof; I couldn't see past the car windows, the world lost to misty grayness. We were in our own world, just the two of us. Nothing else existed past the swirling silver-streaked rain.

"Why did you never write me?" The words came out unbidden. I had wanted to say them for months, but it never felt right. How do you tell someone that he broke your heart when you have to see him everyday after that?

"What?" Shock filled his voice, with just a hint of confusion and anger. His blue eyes darkened in the gray light, but he didn't pull his hand away.

"Why didn't you write me?" I repeated. My voice shook with the effort, but now that it had been asked, I had to finish.

"I did write you. I wrote you so many letters. I went through two Bic pens, and those were hard to get out there. I stopped because you never wrote me. I waited for letters every day, and they never came." He searched my face, the gray light making his dark hair darker and his skin pale.

I frowned, my brow crinkling and my lips tightening, righteous indignation swelling in my chest. I had been so angry at him for never writing for so long, I hadn't realized how much it had hurt. The idea that he thought he stopped because I had never written him was maddening. "I wrote you every day a month! I stopped writing because at the end of that month, the postman handed me back the entire stack of them with "UNDELIVERABLE" stamped on every one. I didn't have any other way to reach you because you never wrote me back."

Dean's mouth opened, his eyes going wide, and he sat back in his seat. He slowly shook his head, trying to make sense of what I just said.

"I looked for you when I came back. I went to the address you gave me, but no one there knew who you were.

The woman in your apartment didn't know anything about any letters. I was sure you had given me the wrong address, or that you had found someone else," he said. He didn't look at me, his voice soft and low. The pain of heartache echoed through his words.

"I didn't find someone else. I got this job with the Saunders and had to move to New York City, but I didn't have any way to tell you since my letters never made it. I checked with my landlord every week though, hoping something would come, and it never did." I didn't want to cry, but I could feel the tears threatening to escape from behind my eyes. I had cried so much over Dean that I thought I didn't have any more tears left, but apparently I did. "Sergeant Dean Sherman of the 101 Airborne Division. I still remember the address."

"That's correct. It probably was just some stupid government secrecy bullshit," Dean said. He closed his eyes for a moment. "Yours was 1281 Simone Drive."

I nodded, and despite my efforts to refrain from crying, a tear found its way down my cheek. I turned and looked out the window so he wouldn't see it. "What did your letters say?"

"What all letters say to someone you love."

Happy heartache washed over me. He *had* loved me.

"Dear Rachel," he read from memory. His voice carried gently over the pounding rain, lulling me with his words. His eyes closed as he recited the letter.

"I know that I've only known you for a short time, but I feel as though I've known you my whole life. Every time you smile, my world brightens and it is that smile that is going to get me through the next few months. Our time together was far too short, but it was the happiest I've ever been."

He paused for a moment, his voice cracking with

emotion as he continued. "You showed me the beauty in the world. You showed me things worth living for. I went back and bought that painting. I've looked at it so many times, and when I see it, I see you. I see all the goodness and light that can come from the dark, and how everything can be beautiful. My world is a better place because of you.

I hope this letter finds you happy and well. Know that I think of you always.

I love you.

Dean."

The tears trickled out down my cheeks. I couldn't speak. Joy, love, despair, and hope all tangled and twisted inside of me. I'd never felt so happy and sad at the same time. I wished I could have had that letter when it was supposed to have been delivered. We would have been together if it had.

Dean turned, his blue eyes bright. With a smooth motion, he reached for me, drawing me into a kiss. The gray world disappeared, replaced by a prism of colors. The shadows and light, the pounding rain, the fear and the heartache- they all faded. Only Dean's lips pressed to mine, his breath on my cheek, his warm hand on my skin were real. The world, and all its problems didn't matter anymore. Dean and this kiss was all that were real. I kissed him like it was the only thing I had ever wanted. I kissed him like I had wanted to kiss him every day since we said goodbye.

I would have kissed him for forever, but a truck zoomed past, shaking the car and honking loudly. Dean and I were startled out of the kiss, noticing that sunlight was now filtering through the car windows. The rain had slowed from the torrential downpour back into a light mist. The sky was lighter and the thunder no longer made the ground shake. Our gray world of rain had dissolved, and we were back in the real world. Dean let go of my hand.

"Dean, I-" I started, my hand touching my lips. I wanted to kiss him again, but now the world could see us.

"I know. I know we can't have that... that this isn't going to work. But I had to kiss you again or my soul was going to break," he said simply. He gave me a halfhearted smile and reached for his seat-belt. His eyes shone with tears, and I knew my cheek was streaked with them. "We should get going."

My heart was breaking again. To be so close to something I had wanted for so long, yet to be so far away, was maddening. He was right, though. Just because we had actually both sent letters, had actually both had feelings, didn't mean we were right for one another. Even if we didn't have the work complication, there was no guarantee we would be able to make it work again. We were both so different, and our feelings were still based on something that happened for a week twenty years ago. It didn't work then, and it wouldn't work now.

I eased the car back out onto the highway, the rain still falling lightly as we headed for the small town in silence. Our kiss still tingled on my lips, my skin still warm from his touch. As we drove, I looked to the sky, praying for rain.

CHAPTER 22

 *resent Day*

I PULLED into the parking lot attached to an old wooden building with small windows that looked exactly like a small town police station in the movies. Dean sat quietly for a moment, as if debating saying something. Inside the darkened glass door with white lettering, I could see a man in a grayish tan uniform sitting at a desk filling out paperwork.

"I'll get the paperwork started while you're at the hospital. I'll call if we finish before you," Dean said. He opened his mouth like he was going to say something more, but instead changed his mind, pushing his lips together and opening the car door. I watched him walk into the station, his movements full of an unconscious deadly grace that can only come with years of practice. His hands opened the door, and I remembered how they had felt on my cheek. I took a deep breath. I couldn't think about that kiss right now, the way his hand cupped my jaw, the sweetness of his tongue... *Stop it! You have work to do!* I chided myself.

The hospital was just a short drive down the main street of the small town. A large building with big windows welcomed patients in, looking more like a hotel than a hospital. It was a new building, and I suspected there was a wing with the Saunders' name on it, but I could never keep track of all the Saunders wings.

I remembered Robbie saying something about it the last time I was in town with him. He kept one of his favorite racing yachts docked at the local marina because he liked the small town feel. The locals had gotten used to him, to the point where he was considered "one of them." It was a good thing too, because he had a tendency to ditch his security, but at least the town was small enough that anyone who didn't belong stuck out like a sore thumb. I had always thought it was a good place for Robbie.

The woman at the main desk sent me up to the second floor to the inpatient unit. The halls were bright and cheery, the smell of fresh wood and paint still lingering in the hallways. It only took me a moment to find the open door into Samantha's room. I could see her sitting in bed reading, her dirty blonde hair up in a ponytail, a bandage on her head and an IV in her arm. I pulled my reading glasses out of their case and carefully centered them on my nose. I knew they made me look more professional, and I actually liked the way they looked. With a deep breath, I knocked and stepped inside.

"Hi, Samantha. I don't know if you remember me, but I would like to talk to you about Robbie," I started, using my business voice. As much as I had liked her when she was a child, this was a business transaction. She gave me a warm smile.

"You're Rachel. Of course I remember you. You would always let Robbie and me stop at the ice cream shop on our way home after sailing lessons. And you are one of the few people that always insisted on calling me Samantha instead of just Sam." She sat up taller in the bed, moving the pillows around to make her more comfortable. I moved to one of the red "leather" padded chairs next to the bed and sat down.

"I'm glad you remember me. I need to talk to you about Robbie, and I'll need you to sign some paperwork." I pulled a folder out of my purse. She looked just like I remembered her. I didn't want to tell her she still looked twelve to me, but to my eyes, she looked exactly the same. Even the ponytail was the same.

"I still can't believe he hit me. I mean, they told me he was drinking, but..." She stopped and shook her head before looking over at me.

I set the folder on the rolling bed table over Samantha's lap, and took out the document inside. I had a computer file full of documents just like it, made up by the Saunders' lawyer for just these kind of situations. I hated that I even had it.

"What happened to him, Rachel? I mean, why would he do that? It's just not like him." Samantha looked over at me, her big gray eyes searching my face. It was those gray eyes that got the two of them ice cream. They were impossible to say no to.

"His dad is dying. He's having a hard time dealing with it. That's not an excuse or a justification, just the explanation. I'd like to ask you not to press charges," I said, indicating the paperwork. "The Saunders family would like to reimburse you for all medical expenses, including any future care you may need with regard to this injury, as well as a payment to cover any work-related expenses this injury may have incurred."

Sam narrowed her eyes, tipping her chin slightly. "And if I said I still wanted to press charges, would I get all the shiny prizes?"

I raised my eyebrows at her. She had always been too smart for her own good as a kid, but at least now it was paying off. I pushed my glasses up on my nose and nodded. "Yes. The Saunders family feels that they should make sure this accident does not end up changing your life. If you still feel the need to press charges and change Robbie's life, then that is purely your decision."

The corner of her mouth twitched upward. "I never intended to press charges against him. Call me sentimental, but I still consider him a friend. I know that he must be going through something crazy hard if he broke his own rule. Besides, he saved me from drowning, so I would like to be able to thank him for that, even if he was the one who put me in the water."

My shoulders dropped, the weight sliding off of them. I knew I had always liked Samantha. "Thank you. I really mean it too, not just as the Saunders' family representative, but as Robbie's friend. Thank you."

"He's my friend. Or at least he was a long time ago. And friends help each other with mistakes. He got me out of trouble a couple of times too." Samantha gave me a grin, almost daring me to ask what kind of trouble. I didn't ask because I didn't want to know; Robbie and Sam were always getting into trouble. "Out of curiosity, how much *is* the payment?"

"Our standard is twenty-five thousand dollars. If you don't think that is going to be enough, I can always speak with the Saunders' lawyer and come up with a more equitable figure." I really didn't want to do that though. The lawyer was good, but he was kind of a jerk.

Samantha went pale and then flushed. "Twenty-five thousand dollars? No, that's fine. That amount is just fine. It's good."

I straightened the paperwork on the table, hiding my smile from her. The amount was obviously more than she had expected. She was still nodding to herself and murmuring that it was fine. A slow look of relief was flooding her features. I wanted so badly to ask what had happened to her since I saw her last, but now was not the appropriate time. This was when I needed to put on my game face and have her sign the papers.

"Excellent. I'm glad that's agreeable. If you'll just sign here... and here... and then fill out this section here, then I can have the medical bills taken care of and the sum wired to your account," I said, handing her a pen. She took it from me, carefully reading the document before she signed. I didn't hide my smile this time. The only other person I knew who read legal documents completely before signing them was Emma, and I was always impressed that she did.

After perusing the document, Samantha signed her name with a flourish in the required areas. Her handwriting was small and neat, and she made sure everything was perfect before handing it back to me. I carefully put the document back in the folder, sliding it into my purse before standing.

"Thank you, Samantha. Can I get you anything before I go?" I asked.

"No thanks," she said, but then her brows tightened and she looked up and made eye contact. "Are you going to go see Robbie?"

I nodded before carefully pocketed my glasses, stowing them in the hard case and slipping them into my purse.

"When you see him, will you tell him I'm all right? And that I'm not angry? I'd really like it if he came and visited me. For old time's sake." She bit her lip. I had always suspected that the two of them had been on the verge of being more than just friends, but this confirmed my suspicions. I wondered for a second what Robbie's life would have been like if she hadn't moved.

"You got it. I'm sure he'll want to see you." I gave her a warm smile, which she quickly returned. "Thank you again, Samantha. I hope I get to see you again soon, though preferably not in the hospital next time."

Samantha laughed, and she settled back into her pillows and book as I left the room. I waved to the nurse at the front desk, humming softly as I walked across the damp asphalt of the parking lot. At least this part of my day was going better than expected.

CHAPTER 23

 *resent Day*

I PARKED CAREFULLY in front of the police station, making sure I was evenly between the two lines. Just because Dean said he knew the sheriff, I didn't want to push my luck. I just wanted to get Robbie out with as little fanfare as possible and get him home to see his father.

The door chimed softly as I walked in. It was a small building, barely more than a room and an office, with two barred cells along the back wall. Sitting in one of them was a very dejected-looking Robbie. He glanced up as I came in, and then put his head back in his hands to stare at the floor. Dean was leaning up against the chest-high wooden monstrosity of a desk, talking with a man in a crisp tan uniform.

"How were things at the hospital?" Dean asked, and all three men looked up to hear my answer.

"Samantha's doing fine. She's agreed not to press

charges," I stated. I heard a low sigh of relief come from the cell. "May I talk with Robbie?"

"Yes, ma'am, you may. Dean and I here just have a few more things to fill out before you three can get on your way." The sheriff gave me a friendly smile. He stood up carefully from the stool behind the desk, limping as he walked to the back cage. As he fit the key into the lock, I glanced at his name tape. Grinswald. I wondered if it was the same Matt Grinswald that was on the beach with Dean and me. I almost asked, but I could wait until after talking to Robbie.

"Hey, Robbie. You sober?" I sat down next to him on the hard wooden bench. He looked miserable. He was wearing a pair of sweatpants that were too big with an oversized SWAT sweatshirt. His light brown hair was messy, and his green eyes were rimmed with red; I couldn't tell if it was from being hung over or from crying.

"Sober. Unfortunately." He sounded absolutely wretched.

"I saw Samantha. She's doing fine, and she wants me to tell you she isn't mad at you." I put my hand on his shoulder. He looked up briefly at my mention of Samantha's name, but his eyes went quickly back to the floor. "Robbie, what's going on? What are you doing?"

"I'm sitting here listening to the rain," he said. I frowned.

"That's not what I meant and you know it. You're better than this," I said, gesturing to the jail cell.

"It doesn't matter. I'm always going to be the fuck-up. That's my lot in life." His back bristled under my fingers, but I kept my hand on him.

"It's only your lot in life if you make it that. I've seen you sail, Robbie. I've seen drive and determination in you that would make Jack look like an indecisive toddler. You're better than this," I told him. I meant every word. If he could only see how he shone when he was sailing; if the world were a boat, he would be president, prime minister, and king. I wished he could see what I saw in him.

"Unfortunately, you're the only one who thinks that." Robbie looked up at me, his eyes angry and hurt. "My dying father thinks I'll never amount to anything, my brother's a billionaire CEO, and my mother's a harpy. What the hell am I supposed to do?"

I sighed. My heart was breaking for him. All I could see as I kept my hand on his back was the scared little boy I took home from his first sailing lesson. Maybe it was because I had just seen Samantha, or maybe it was the smell of the water in the air, but to my eyes, he was just a little boy. I rubbed his back, trying to think of how to convince him that he was better than he thought. I had tried to keep my eye on him when he was a boy, but Jack had been my real responsibility. I tried my best, but there wasn't a way for me to be in two places at once.

Dean rapped gently on the bars, catching both our attention. "The sheriff has agreed to drop all charges."

The sheriff's keys jangled as he opened the door, releasing the two of us into the office. As I walked by Dean, I whispered, "That must be some favor he owed you."

"Nothing much," Dean said with a shrug. He put a strong hand on Robbie's shoulder, guiding him toward the exit. "All right, Robbie, let's get you home before anyone notices we were gone."

Robbie stopped cold. "Dad doesn't know I'm here?"

"No. No one but Dean and I know you're here. Well, and Emma, but that's just because she's covering for us. And you know she'd never tell."

Robbie blushed. The anger seemed to wash out of him, his back going straighter and with more power and confidence in his stride. He wasn't going home to meet the firing squad anymore.

"Robert Saunders. I just need you to sign here and you'll be free to go," the sheriff said, catching Robbie's attention. Robbie quickly picked up a pen and started signing the papers laid out on the desk as Dean pointed to the various places that needed a signature.

I looked over at the sheriff, seeing his name tape again. The hair was the right shade of blonde, and the eyes seemed familiar. It was when he smiled at me that I knew it was Matt. The smile was exactly the same.

"Yes, Rachel, I'm that Matt Grinswald," he said with a laugh. I felt my cheeks redden at being caught.

"I didn't think you recognized me. It's been a long time." I leaned up against the desk, feeling very young with Dean and Matt both standing there.

"I wouldn't have if Dean hadn't said your name. You look the same-- I just never thought I'd see any of you girls again. How is Jenny?" he asked. His pitch raised on Jenny's name and I wondered if he missed her as much as Dean and I had missed one another.

"She's doing well. She ended up marrying her high school sweetheart, but it didn't work out. They got divorced about two years ago, but she's got three amazing kids that I get to play "aunt" too. I'll tell her you said hi next time I see her," I said with a smile. Matt beamed.

"Please do. I'd love to buy her a drink sometime." The big sheriff picked up Robbie's finished paperwork and flipped through it. "Everything looks in order. Out you go, Robbie. I don't want to see you in here again, understand?"

"Yes, sir. I'll only be in here to be the bail-er, not the bail-ee," Robbie said with a small grin. The sheriff cracked a smile and nodded.

"Thanks, Grinswald. Beers on Thursday?" Dean asked as Robbie opened the main door.

A loud, "Of course!" followed us out of the station as Grinswald clapped Dean on the back. Robbie and I settled into the car, Robbie taking the backseat, and it was only a moment before Dean joined us.

"I didn't know Matt was so close nearby," I said as I started the car. The engine purred as we headed back down the highway.

"Yeah, he was transferred up here last fall. It's nice to have one of the guys close by." Dean looked out the window and I knew he was thinking about Frontera. I wished he could have made it too. "What ever happened to Jenny and Kimberly? You said Jenny got a divorce?"

I nodded, smiling at him. This wasn't something we had ever talked about since we started working together, and it felt nice. "Jenny lives in Jersey with her kids now. Kimberly is in LA. She works in the movies and does some of her own painting on the side."

"Are they happy?" Dean asked quietly. I could feel his eyes on me, their blue drawing me to them.

"Relatively." It was a complicated answer. They all were happy for the most part, though.

Dean nodded and crossed his legs again, staring out the window at the oncoming evening. The sun was just beginning to creep into the horizon, hints of starlight starting to peek through the silver clouds. I watched the road, the black asphalt flying beneath our wheels as we sped back to our real lives, but all I wanted was to find that rainstorm world so I could be alone with Dean again.

CHAPTER 24

 *resent Day*

ROBBIE PASSED me as I walked down the hallway toward Daniel's room. His eyes were still rimmed with red, and his lips were pursed together as he walked the ornate carpet, his mind lost in thought. I don't think he even saw me as he paced back and forth down the long hallway. I wasn't sure he had even been in to see his father since we had brought him home, but at least he was in the house.

I knocked softly before entering the large room that had become Daniel's infirmary. A large hospital bed took up the center of the room, an oxygen tank and an IV pole tucked carefully beside them. Bianca sat in a large easy chair in the corner, her feet tucked up under her as she typed on her laptop. I could hear soft classical music, playing softly in the background. Knowing Daniel, it was probably Mozart.

Daniel sat propped up in the bed, pillows and blankets tucked tightly around him. His pale face was so gaunt that his eyes seemed to sink into his paper thin skin. I remembered the healthy father whom had welcomed me into the Saunders' household. Where thick brown hair had once fallen into his eyes with a roguish flare, white wisps hung flat against his head. He smiled as I entered, his lips thin and pale.

"How you doing, old man?" I asked, sitting next to the large bed. Daniel looked perturbed, but his eyes were twinkling.

"I *was* going to go dancing, but Bianca says her feet hurt," he answered. Bianca snorted from her chair, a smile crossing her face. They had loved to dance.

"Well, I guess I'll just have to get her new shoes for tomorrow night." I reached for his hand, squeezing it gently. I could feel the bones through his parchment-like skin.

"Robert came to see me today. I mean, Robbie. He hates it when I call him Robert," Daniel said, a smile forming on his lips. He had a fascination with the Kennedys, and had always thought his children would grow up to do great things like their namesakes. "I had him tell me all about his last race. I'm sad I didn't get to see it. It sounded like a marvelous race. He said he won, but it was close the whole time. He says he has another one coming up in two weeks."

But Daniel won't get to see it. The words hung unspoken in the air like acrid smoke. It was an offhand comment, but we all knew he would never see his son race again. The silence was thick and uncomfortable. Daniel cleared his throat and adjusted the oxygen tube to his nose, trying to break the sudden tension.

"So, Rachel, what are you doing this evening? Going dancing, I hope?" Daniel changed the topic. I knew he wanted everyone to be happy. He had accepted his death, and was going gracefully. It was the rest of us that were having a hard time.

"Jack's given me the night off, but I thought I would just hang around here. I have work to catch up on," I said. Daniel frowned.

"Young lady, I will not have you hanging around here waiting for me to die. I promise I won't go tonight. Go out. Go dancing. I want to know you are having a fun evening, not moping around here. I'm tired of everyone putting their lives on hold waiting for me. So get out of here, and go have some fun." It would have been a marvelous speech, except his voice gave out and he began coughing at the end. I held onto his hand, watching his thin body shake.

Bianca stood, walking quickly to the oxygen tank and upping the flow. It hissed like an angry snake, but Daniel managed to take deeper breaths, his body settling back to normal. I looked away from him, noticing the pictures on the nightstand next to the oxygen tank. There was the picture of Jack and Daniel playing football in the hand-crafted frame from that Father's Day long ago. The colors were worn and faded, the frame obviously having been displayed for many years. Next to it was a picture of a smiling Robbie and Daniel on a small sailing vessel. A picture of the two boys sitting on my lap reading a Dr. Seuss book occupied another frame. The last one was an old black and white picture of Bianca blowing him a kiss. A lump grew in my throat. I didn't know how Bianca managed to do this without bursting into tears at every moment. She was a strong woman.

Bianca smiled at her husband as the coughing stopped, running her fingers along his cheek. He looked up at her with adoration in his eyes, catching her hand and kissing it gently. She bent and kissed him back on his forehead before going back and sitting in her chair, watching him with loving eyes.

"If it will make you feel better, I'll go out." I would do anything to make him happy. "There's a restaurant I've been wanting to try," I lied. There was no restaurant. I wasn't even hungry, but I knew he wanted to see me go out and enjoy myself.

"Good. And don't think you can just hide downstairs. I'll send Dean after you and have him drag you to that restaurant kicking and screaming." He gave me one of his no-nonsense looks and I couldn't help but smile.

"That will be hard because it's Dean's night off too," I said. I stuck my tongue out at him.

"Oh, it is?" Daniel gave me a questioning look, but before I could read into it he shrugged and added, "Then I'll just have to send Bianca and Emma. They may not be able to lift you as easily, but between the two of them, I think they could at least get you tied up and in the car."

Bianca gave a girlish giggle. "Please, we'd even get her tied to the chair at the restaurant." I smiled at the image of the older woman wrapping me with rope like an old vaude-ville villain while Emma carried me into the car, the two of them cackling and twirling at their mustaches.

"Go out. Have a good time tonight. Please, it will make me feel better knowing that one of us is having a fun evening." He looked up at me, his eyes still bright despite the paleness of his face. I couldn't say no to him.

"All right. I'll go. I'm bringing you back some dessert, though." I gave him a firm look, and he laughed.

I stood up and headed toward the door. As I stepped outside, Bianca called out after me, "Make sure it's something chocolate!" I could hear Daniel laughing as I closed the door.

CHAPTER 25

*resent Day*

I HAD INTENDED to go to a rustic Italian restaurant just a few miles from the Saunders' mansion. I had intended to walk in, sit down, eat lasagna and tiramisu, have a glass of wine, and then head back and take a long hot shower. That was what I had intended. Instead, I was standing in front of Dean's apartment building.

I could see a light coming from his corner unit, the yellow window shining cheerfully into the dark night. The wind blew across the yard, rattling the remaining leaves on the trees and making the fallen ones skitter across the sidewalk. The moon hung low, orange and full against the night sky. I was about to go back to my car, to drive to that little restaurant and actually do what I was supposed to do, but the memory of that kiss pulled at me. Now that we had kissed, even just once, I wanted more.

Before I even knew what I was doing, my hand was

knocking at his door. I looked down at the brave appendage in shock, wondering what the hell I was thinking. I needed to go home. I needed to leave this where it was. The wind blew my hair out of its bun, but I couldn't find the rubber-band, so I just smoothed it down. No good was going to come of this, only heartache. *I should turn around and run back to my car and just leave him thinking it was some doorbell ditch*, I thought.

The door opened, allowing the warm light to spill out into the dark. He stood there, wearing only pajama pants. My mouth went wet, then immediately dry at the sight of his bare chest, the muscles taut and hard. The eagle tattoo looked exactly the same, but now there was a scar from the bullet wound above the eagle's head. His nipples hardened as the night air hit them, and I had to force my eyes away from their perfection.

"Rachel? What are you doing here?" he asked softly. His brows came together and he stepped out to put his hands on my shoulders. "Is everything all right?"

A red-hot blush seared up my neck. He was worried something had happened to Daniel. I was here because I couldn't stop thinking about his kiss, not because anything was wrong. I suddenly didn't know what to say.

"Here, come inside. It's cold out there." He ushered me into his home, carefully shutting out the night behind me. "Let me throw on a shirt. I'll be right back. Make yourself comfortable."

He disappeared into a small room off to the left that I assumed was his bedroom. The apartment was comfortably furnished. A brown leather sofa and recliner faced a huge TV, a gas fireplace's flame dancing merrily underneath it. A small, heavy wooden table with two chairs sat in the kitchen, but it was covered in mail and random odds and ends. Canvas paintings hung on every wall. The one on the mantle I even suspected might be a Renoir. The man loved his art.

"Is everything okay?" Dean now wore a light gray T-shirt with the DS Oil and Gas logo emblazoned on the the front. It was easier to think without his muscles tempting me to touch them. The kitchen smelled delicious, and I could see something boiling on the stove. I felt guilty for disrupting his night off. "Please, take off your jacket and stay awhile. You hungry? I made my favorite beef stew and I always make too much."

I carefully took off my shoes, placing them neatly by the door and setting my jacket on top of them. "I don't mean to intrude. I'm not really even sure why I'm even here. I meant to go to this Italian restaurant, but I missed the exit, and I don't even remember turning off the highway. Suddenly, I was in your parking lot." A fresh blush crept up the back of my neck and into my scalp. Somehow, I was as nervous as a girl on a first date.

Dean laughed, a hearty and wonderful sound. "I'm actually glad you came by. It means I can stop picking up the phone every five minutes to try and get the courage to call you. Soup?"

"Yes, please. It smells wonderful," I said, stepping into his bright kitchen. Everything was organized and meticulous, except for the couple of spots where the soup had splattered onto the stove. He lifted the lid and ladled out a delicious looking stew into a large green bowl, handing the full bowl into my waiting hands.

"Here you go. Careful, it's hot. It's a recipe I learned from one of the Army cooks and then made into my own. It isn't fancy, but it sure tastes good." He gave me one of his perfect lopsided grins as he handed me a spoon. His smile made the butterflies begin to dance in my stomach again. "We can sit on the couch."

While he poured himself a bowl, I headed over to the brown leather sofa. It was worn and soft, giving the entire room a comfortable feeling. I balanced the bowl on my lap and raised a spoonful to my mouth. Flavor rushed across my tongue, the beef and vegetables combining with just enough spice to make my mouth water for more.

"This is delicious!" I took another bite, savoring the meaty broth and the bits of potatoes and carrots. "I didn't know you could cook."

Dean sat down on the couch next to me, close enough to make my heart speed up, but far enough away to be considered proper. "I can't really cook. This is probably the only thing I know how to make, but I just *really* know how to make it."

I took another bite of the hearty stew, enjoying just sitting next to Dean. I felt like I was floating on air, my nerves frazzled and excited. *It's just Dean*, I told myself, but that was the problem. I had tried to ignore it, but today's kiss had hammered it home. I still loved him. He made me feel safe and warm, yet adventurous and exciting all at the same time. I peeked a glance over at him as he blew on his soup, his mouth making a perfect, kissable circle. I wondered if I made him feel the same way.

Before I knew it, I was scraping the bottom of the bowl. I looked down at it, surprised. I hadn't even realized I was hungry. It was the first time I had finished a meal all week. Dean looked over and grinned at my empty bowl.

"Looks like you liked it." Pride at his cooking rippled through his voice. I smiled. It had been fantastic. "Do you want some more? I have plenty."

"Maybe in a little bit. I can't believe I ate all of it. It was wonderful." I handed him my bowl and he grinned at my praise. He sauntered into the kitchen and I had to focus to keep from watching his perfect ass. The pajama pants did nothing to hide that it was as muscular as the rest of his body.

"Can I get you a drink?" he called from the kitchen.

"Um, sure. What do you have?" I asked, stretching my arms out above my head. The soft leather creaked as I stood up and followed him to the kitchen.

He was standing in his pantry, frowning at a bottle in his hands. He turned and held it up for me to see. "It looks like all I have is this champagne," he apologized. "I haven't been home for a while, and this is all I have." I noticed the repetition. He sounded a little nervous.

I took the bottle and looked at the label. It was definitely something left over from a wedding or even a New Year's Eve party, but it still sounded good. I handed it back and smiled. "Works for me."

With deliberate fingers, he unwrapped the foil and twisted the thin metal holding the cork. I jumped when the cork flew out into his waiting kitchen towel. He laughed gently and grinned at my surprise.

"Glasses are in that cabinet there," he said, gesturing with his head to one of the wooden doors. I opened it to find a neat row of glassware, and pulled out two slender glasses and set them on the counter next to him. He poured the bubbling golden liquid, and we each picked one up.

"What should we toast to?" Dean asked. He raised his glass, stopping just short of tapping mine.

"To old friends," I answered. He smiled at the similarity to our first toast with champagne.

"To old friends," he said softly, and we clinked our glasses and took a sip. I closed my eyes and was transported back in time, back to the night I met Dean. The champagne even tasted the same.

Dean was so close to me that I could feel his body heat radiating toward me. His head bent slightly so he leaned over me, the two of us almost pressed together in the small kitchen. My heart pounded in my chest, a light-headed happiness filling me up like a cup. Every fiber of my being prayed he would just lean forward a little bit more, just enough for our lips to touch. I rose onto my toes, straining to bridge the distance between us, to kiss him again.

He stepped back, his lips pressed into a thin line. "Rachel, we can't..." He looked at me, his eyes full of desire but pleading with me, as if they just wanted me to understand.

I set the glass down, smoothing my hair into it's normal tight bun, finding a spare hair-tie in my pocket. He was being the responsible one. He was the one making sure we didn't do something we were going to regret later. I hung my head, a blush searing through my cheeks.

"I'm sorry, Dean. I shouldn't have come." I turned and headed toward the door, biting my lip to keep the emotions bottled up. I could let them out once I was in the car, but I didn't want him to see me break. "Thank you for the lovely dinner."

I was two steps away from the door when his hand caught my wrist. He pulled gently, spinning me into his chest and wrapping his arms around me. His lips pressed into mine, full of need and want. I opened my mouth, his tongue slipping in and finding mine. He tasted better than anything I could have imagined.

Dean's body pressed into mine, his muscles hard and flexed as he held me to him, his gentle hands holding the back of my neck and pulling me into him. I moaned softly, the years of wanting him surging to the surface.

"Please don't go," he whispered as we both stopped to breathe. Our foreheads were pressed together, and we both took big, unsteady breaths. I couldn't have left if I wanted to. "Never leave again."

I kissed him again, wrapping my arm around his neck as he wrapped his arms around my waist. It was a hungry, desperate kiss, full of years of lost desire. I wanted him more than I had ever wanted anything in my life. And he was right there, kissing me back, asking me to stay. I felt a tear trickle down my cheek, but it was one of pure joy.

My hand went to the bottom of his shirt and pulled upward. I had wanted to touch those muscles from the moment he had opened the door. He casually raised it over his head and flung it to the floor. His blue eyes twinkled in the light of the kitchen as I ran my fingers across his flesh. He let his head fall back with a low moan. I leaned forward and kissed his hardening nipples, tasting them like candy. His skin was delicious.

Without warning, Dean scooped me up. I wrapped my arms around his neck and kissed him, drinking him in as he carried me to the bedroom. His muscles were hard and strong underneath me, and he never struggled with my weight, moving across the room as though I were light as a feather.

He set me down carefully on the tall bed, never letting the kiss between us stop. My fingers ran up and down his arms and back, desperate to touch every inch of his skin. He broke free of my kiss, pulling back and looking me over as I lay on his bed. He smiled appreciatively.

"God, you're beautiful," he whispered. He blinked as though he hadn't actually intended to say it out loud. I was glad for the dark in the room as a satisfied blush flared across my cheeks.

"Even now?" I asked quietly. I knew I wasn't the girl I had been twenty years ago, and part of me was afraid he would see only the changes.

He leaned forward, his eyes dark and full of barely contained lust. "Especially now."

His hands went to the top button of my dress shirt. His lips twitched up to one side in a cocky grin as he slowly unbuttoned, moving down to the next as soon as it was free. He leaned forward, kissing the newly revealed skin, savoring it. With every kiss, the spark of desire burned brighter within me. At the rate I was going, I was going to be a raging inferno of lust by the time he got my shirt off.

With delicious slowness, he worked his way to the last button, opening the shirt and running his fingers along my skin. A low moan of pure want escaped my lips. With every touch, every look he was igniting flames along my nerves.

His fingers traced lazy circles across my stomach, slowly creeping lower and lower to the band of my pants. The button opened easily, and I lifted my hips as he tugged gently on my pants. He continued with his policy of kissing every inch of skin bared to him, his tongue grazing the soft flesh of my thigh down to my calves.

I leaned my head back into the pillow, losing myself to the sensation. His teeth nibbled on the tender fold of my knee, his breath hot on my exposed skin. I lay on the bed, bare but for my panties, bra, and open shirt. Every touch sent a thrill straight into the core of my body.

Dean worked his way back up my legs, his soft kisses tickling the sensitive skin of my inner thigh. I sat up, taking his chin in my fingers and bringing him in to kiss my mouth. I needed his kiss. His fingers slipped the shirt from my shoulders, and he escaped my hungry mouth to kiss their bare tops. I moaned, tangling my fingers in his short hair.

One graceful finger slid along the length of my bra strap, tracing the lacy fabric down across the tops of my breasts. I was breathing hard, my chest rising and falling with his finger. A shiver of anticipation rolled through me.

He leaned forward and kissed the top of my right breast. My heart fluttered in my chest, the primal ache growing harder to resist. I wanted his body so badly I could taste it, but I didn't want to stop. His every touch was a drug, and I was hooked.

Dean's warm hand caressed my side, tracing the bra to the back clasp. He struggled with it for a moment, finally making a frustrated noise as the clasp refused to yield. He looked up at me, his disappointment and insurmountable need pouring over me. My breath caught at his gaze, the sheer volume of desire catching me off guard.

I giggled, twisting my hands behind me to do it myself. I felt the wire release, and slowly, I lowered the lacy fabric. I bit my lip, watching Dean's face as the fabric fell away. His eyes dilated and his mouth opened in wordless appreciation. His eyes met mine, dark and hungry. I was vibrating with want for him.

With that perfect half-smile, he reached past my ear, snagging the hair-band holding my hair. My hair fell from the makeshift bun in dark waves around my shoulders. Dean hissed with appreciation, making me feel like the most beautiful creature on the face of the earth.

"So damn beautiful," he murmured. His mouth found my breast, gently pushing me back onto the pillow with his hand. His tongue strummed the pink flesh like a guitar string, sending beautiful vibrations through my body. I pressed his head into my chest, arching my back to give him better access.

A jolt of pleasure surged through me as his fingers found my pleasure center. He made slow circles on the outside of my light pink panties, revving my internal engines to full power. I lost all sense of time and space. The only thing that existed was Dean and my pleasure. It wasn't long before the sheer intensity of the fire burning within me overcame all my senses. Ecstasy rolled through me in waves, pure bliss washing through every fiber of my being.

When I could breathe again, I reached for him. I didn't want to wait any longer. I craved him. I needed him. I had needed him for so long and I didn't have to wait any longer. I clawed at his pants, desperate to have him. He laughed as he wiggled free, showing me that he didn't have anything on underneath. No wonder his ass had looked so good.

He stood before, bathed in soft moonlight. He moved to the nightstand, fishing a small square packet from a corner drawer and hastily putting it on. He didn't want to wait any longer either.

He was between my legs in less than a moment, his masculine scent heady and intoxicating. I could feel his massive manhood pressing against me, seeking entrance, and as we made eye contact, he entered.

My body sang with pleasure. I cried out his name, feeling the two of us finally joining as one. We were no longer separate or alone. We were together. I gripped the headboard, feeling my knuckles go white as he delved deeply into me. My back arched with every thrust, wanting to take him ever deeper inside of me.

Our eyes never left one another. His winter-blue eyes peered into my soul, the two of us speaking volumes without words. He kissed me softly, his lips gentle yet insistent for more. My body was on fire for his touch, the ache unbearable. I wrapped my legs around him, and with all my strength rolled to the side.

He made a surprised growl, but grinned as he saw me straddle him. He moved his hands to the headboard, groaning softly as I began to writhe up and down, sliding and enjoying every inch of him. His face contorted into a mask of pleasure, his arms tensing as I found a rhythm.

I could barely stand it, the pleasure of having him inside me coursing through me in waves. Every centimeter, every touch was something I had craved. I had dreamed of this for twenty years, and the reality was so much better than the fantasy.

I slowed my pace and leaned down to kiss him. As if waiting for his moment, he wrapped his arms around me and flipped me back onto my back. I didn't mind, though. I loved looking up, seeing his arms and chest flexing above me and the way his waist tapered into a delicious V. His hips rocked back and forth, sending undulations of pleasure into me.

His pace quickened, his breathing coming in shallow pants. His eyes drifted closed as sweet climax washed over him. I cried out, and Dean's low ragged answering groan filled my ears. I clung to him, pulling him into me, never wanting him to leave. I felt his release wash over the inside of my body. With slowing strokes, he shuddered and his body relaxed.

Moments later, he rolled to his side, his eyes searching my face. Happiness like I hadn't seen in years spread across his features. He brushed the hair out of my eyes, smiling as he kissed me. My world was perfect.

The dark night wrapped the two of us like a warm blanket. I could hear the fire crackle in the other room. Dean was solid beside me, his arms wrapped tight around me as though he were afraid I might run off into the night. I never wanted to leave.

The moon peeked through the window, casting the room in silver shadows. The light danced across the sheets, turning them into an ocean of pleasure, and the air sparkled with promise. A single moonbeam soared through the window, landing on a small painting on Dean's nightstand. I sat up on my elbow, peering over him to look at it. It was the painting from the beach.

"What are you looking at?" Dean asked. His voice was rough and incredibly sexy. A shiver of desire went up my spine, and I kissed his cheek before leaning over and picking it up. He cocked his head, a boyish grin on his face as my chest passed in front of his face, but I managed to pick up the painting and settle back into the nook of his arm.

"I can't believe you still have this," I said softly, tracing the dark lines of the silhouette. He cuddled me in closer to him, his lips against my hair.

"I told you, I went back and got it. It's my favorite work of art." His breath tickled against my cheek.

"Even more than the Renoir on your mantle?" I asked. I had a feeling it was real, but if it wasn't, it was still expertly done. If it was real, it was worth a fortune.

"Even more than the Renoir." He kissed me softly. "I only have a love of art because you gave it to me."

"I love you, Dean." The words came out easily, as though I had always said them. In my heart, I had said them every day since I had met him.

He squeezed me tighter, his arms strong and safe. "I love you, too." he whispered. No words had ever felt so good. Happiness and contentment surged through every inch of my being. Things felt right in the world. He nuzzled my hair, kissing me gently. I nestled into the crook of his arm, resting my ear against his chest. His heart beat in my ear, rhythmic and soothing.

"I can hear your heart beat," I whispered.

"It beats for you. It always has," he whispered back. I smiled, closing my eyes and simply enjoying being with the love of my life. Dean's heart pulsed, my own heart matching his mesmerizing rhythm as I drifted off to sleep.

 *resent Day*

I woke up the next morning to find that Dean was already out of bed. The room seemed empty without him. I glanced at the painting on the nightstand, the woman still defiant against the storm after all these years. It made me smile that he had kept it.

The floor was cold to my bare feet as I stumbled into the bathroom. Sitting on the toilet seat was a clean pair of sweats and a plain gray t-shirt. I slid the comfortable clothing on, rolling the waist band to keep the pants up. The shirt smelled like Dean, and I breathed it in, enjoying the scent. I giggled as I realized there was no way he was going to get this t-shirt back. Well, maybe, when it lost that wonderful smell and needed refreshing.

The rest of the apartment was quiet, but I found a pot of coffee ready with a note in Dean's messy handwriting.

> *Good morning Beautiful,*
> *I didn't want to wake you, but I'm getting breakfast. Creamer's in the fridge.*
> *I love you.*

I folded the note and stuck it in my pocket. Even though it was just a simple message, it felt dear to me. Maybe it was because I had wanted simple notes like this, simple mornings like this, for a very, very long time.

The creamer was about the only thing in the fridge. That and a jar of pickles. When he said he hadn't been home much, he wasn't kidding. I poured a cup of coffee and wandered over to the couch, sipping at the dark liquid. Dean had good taste in coffee. I could get used to spending mornings here. Maybe he would even give me a drawer to keep my things in.

The thought of getting to fall asleep wrapped up in Dean's arms and then wake up in the morning and have breakfast, made me giddy. In my mind I could see the two of us getting ready for work together...

Work was a problem. Dread settled in the pit of my stomach. We could both be fired for this. I could hear Daniel's voice, repeating the conversation we had when Dean was hired.

> *"Thank you for telling me about your prior relationship with this man. You understand that I have to enforce the employee contract. If I make an exception for you, I will have to make exceptions for others. The whole point of the employee contract was to negate that issue,"* Daniel said. He stood tall in his office. There were boxes on the desk, though, the first sign that his

illness was forcing him to hand the reigns over to Jack.

"I don't think it will be a problem. I don't see the two of us getting back together. I just felt it was important to tell you. I didn't want it to come up later and be an issue." I stood straight and tall in front of his desk. I had been afraid that he would be angry.

"Oh, Rachel." He gave me a big smile and came around the desk, putting his hands on my shoulders. "You are allowed to have a life outside of this company. In fact, I'd love it if you met someone and made me a godfather. I think you'll find someone better than a washed up soldier to make you happy, so I'm not going to waver on this."

"I understand. I really don't think it's going to be a problem. Those feelings, I don't think they'll ever be what they were before," I said. It was true. I was sure after our interview that he hated my guts.

He hugged me then, his arms strong as he squeezed me close. "You are the daughter I never had. I really do just want you to be happy."

How were we going to make this work? I knew after last night, I would never be content to just sit back and watch him. Now that Dean was in my life, now that we were together, I couldn't give him up. We could try and hide our relationship, but sooner or later it would come out and one, or both, of us would be out of a job. The contract was clear.

Irrational fears started to fly through my brain. We were both going to be fired and we would end up homeless on the street. *Jack would never let that happen, and even if it did, at least you'd still be together*, the little voice in my head whispered.

I sagged into the couch. The leather was soft and smelled good, but I didn't cuddle into it. I knew I was just waiting for the universe to rip us apart again. My heart was a mess. It had broken when he left me the first time. It had broken when I hired him and had to ignore him. Now it was breaking because I was going to have to lose him. It was either lose him or lose the job and the people I considered a family with it.

A tear trickled down my cheek. This roller coaster of emotions was going to drive me insane. I wiped at my cheek angrily. This was getting me no where. Sitting here and crying because some stupid employee contract said that I couldn't date the man of my dreams was ridiculous. I wasn't going to just sit around and let him get away from me again. I was going to talk to Jack. I was going to fix this. There was no reason for me to be upset. No reason for us to go through the pain of losing one another again for something as equally trivial as the last time.

The sound of the front door opening pulled me from my thoughts. Dean gave me a huge grin as he walked in the door, the smell of food wafting out of a paper bag. I quickly changed my expression, putting on a happy face. I wanted us to be happy. I didn't want him to worry about his job, or mine. I just wanted to enjoy this morning. I silenced the voices of worry. *Just enjoy what you have.*

Dean kissed the top of my head, my hair messy around my shoulders. The couch creaked softly as he sat next to me. He pushed one of the dark brown strands behind my ear and gave me a kiss on the nose. "Now, let's have some breakfast. I got those English muffin sandwiches I know you like."

I couldn't help but smile as he reached for the paper bag with the food inside. He handed me a paper wrapped sandwich, the smells of egg and cheese making my mouth water. I was hungrier than I had thought.

I was half-way through my sandwich, leaning against Dean in a happy silence, ignoring the warning in my heart, when my phone started to ring. I still had an hour before I was expected to be back at work, but I hurried over to my purse to pick it up.

"Rachel! Oh, thank heaven," Emma cried into the phone. "I was so afraid I wasn't going to reach you in time."

"Emma, what's happening?" A note of panic crept into my voice.

"It's Daniel. He's not doing well. And he's asking for you. You need to come soon." I could practically hear the tears running down her face. She loved the old man. I felt the phone tremble in my hand.

"I'll be there in just a couple of minutes."

"Okay. Hurry," Emma said. I clicked off the phone and stared at it for a moment.

Dean took my hands in his. "I'll drive you. Let's go."

CHAPTER 27

resent Day

I PULLED my hair up into a bun as Dean parked the car in front of the Saunders' mansion. Even from here I could tell something was wrong. The feeling of a string about to be cut vibrated out of the house. Dark shadows cast up onto the porch, the autumn morning sun still cold. I shivered and pulled a sweater up around my shoulders.

I stepped out of the car, making sure my shirt hung straight. I always carried a change of clothes in my car. In my line of work, you never knew when you would be stuck at the office overnight. Or sleeping at your boyfriend's place for the first time.

Emma hurried out to greet us. She ran barefoot across the wet grass, the hem on her pants growing darker with every step. She hugged her arms around her, keeping herself warm as well as from falling apart. Tear stains already streaked her face. She didn't even bat an eyelash at the fact that we had arrived together, instead grabbing my hand and hurrying me toward the house.

"What happened, Emma? Is he..." I asked. A lump in my throat had started forming the instant she had called, and it hadn't stopped growing. I didn't want to be late. I had to say goodbye.

"No, he's still here. He woke up early and started having trouble breathing. The oxygen wasn't helping anymore, and we got the doctor... he says it won't be long now." Emma choked on the last few words, her voice failing her.

I stopped in my tracks, pulling Emma in for a hug. She clung to me like a child, her bare feet cold on the wooden porch, her sobs shaking her body. I held her, my own heart numb. I had dreaded this day for months. If not for the cold wind making Emma's hair whip against my face, I would have thought it a bad dream. It didn't feel real.

Dean opened the main door, making it creak and shaking us out of our hug. A tension was floating through the house, like the calm before a storm; I knew we didn't have much time. We hurried into the house, Dean a solid presence behind us. I knew he wasn't close to Daniel, but the two women in his life were. Emma and I bounded up the main staircase, my fear of losing him before I got to say goodbye spurring me to go faster.

I slowed once I reached the door. Bianca was sitting on the floor outside his room. She looked as though a giant child had simply set her down after playing with her like a doll. Bianca's blonde hair was perfectly coiffed, her pantsuit pressed and neat, but her legs splayed out in front of her and her eyes stared, unseeing. Jack had her hand in his as he knelt beside her, whispering soft words to try and move her to a chair nearby. She just kept shaking her head and staring into space.

I swallowed against the tears that threatened to rise out of my chest. If I wasn't careful, it felt as though a sob would just explode out of me, so I kept it inside, feeling its claws rip me apart. Dean placed his hand on my shoulder. It was a small gesture, but just having him beside me was enough to give me strength. I didn't know what I would do if I didn't have him there. Emma hurried to Jack's side, taking Bianca's other hand and pulling gently. Between the two of them, they managed to get her into a high-backed chair next to the door.

The door was cracked open, and I peeked inside. Jack shook his head, warning me not to go inside yet. I could see Robbie kneeling by the head of his father's bed. Daniel's hand rested on his shoulder, a soft smile across his thin lips. Robbie's shoulders shook slightly, and Daniel motioned him to come closer. I watched as Daniel whispered something into Robbie's ear, Robbie's spine going stiff. From my vantage point, I could see Daniel smile, pulling his son toward him for a hug with weak arms.

Robbie leaned into his father for a moment, a sob shaking out of his chest, but then broke away and ran blindly for the door. I stepped aside before he could hit me on his way out, tears streaking his face. A mask of pain twisted his features as he hurried to a space down the hall. He wanted to run out the door, run away from the pain, but something held him firm to the hallway, so he paced it like a caged animal.

I watched him for a moment, wondering what Daniel could have said to make him react like that. My heart ached for the boy. There was so much pain today. I wanted to chase after him, to hold him in my arms like I did when he was small and tell him it was going to be all right. I knew that wasn't what he wanted right now, though, so I stayed by the door.

"Rachel," Daniel called weakly. I turned to see him smiling at me through the open door. I stepped inside, closing the door behind me firmly. Everyone in the hallway had already spoken with him, and I wanted a moment alone with the man I considered a father.

"Hi, Daniel," I said. My voice trembled on his name. He patted the bedspread beside him, his hand struggling at the simple motion. The room seemed immensely large as I crossed it, and Daniel, suddenly tiny in his huge bed. I sat down, taking his hand in both of mine.

"Rachel, you know I love you like a daughter? I've only ever wanted what was best for my children, and it seems I've failed all of them in some way. I'm hoping that I can change some of that." He stopped, a fit of coughing overtaking him. Death stalked the corners of the room. I waited until he regained his breath before speaking.

"You've never failed me, Daniel. You're the closest and best thing I've ever had to a father. I'm proud that you consider me one of your own," I said. A tear trickled down my cheek, and I wiped it away with the back of my hand.

Daniel gave me a weak smile. The light was fading from his eyes. They looked clouded and distant, as if the spark was fading. He looked at me, but he was seeing through me. "There should be love in your life. He's good for you, Rachel. I wish I could have seen it earlier, but the two of you complement one another. He is the shadow to your light. Neither one is complete without the other," he whispered.

"I don't understand." I shook my head and felt another tear escape. This one I didn't even bother wiping.

"You don't have to. Just an old man rambling on his deathbed." His eyes focused back on me. "I love you, Rachel, as I love all my children." His breath caught again, his lungs struggling for air, but his body was so weak the bed didn't even tremble with his effort. I held his hand, unable to do anything. When it stopped again, he squeezed my hand and smiled. "Will you send in my wife? She's been my constant for my entire life. Everyone deserves a love like ours. Something that will never end."

I nodded, sniffling back my tears. With shaking hands, I released his bony one, placing it gently on the white bedspread. I kissed his forehead, and one of my tears dripped off my cheek and onto his pillow. He closed his eyes and smiled up at me. His face was losing the lines of pain, paling as he came closer to finding relief.

I opened the door, leaning heavily against the doorframe. My mind was nothing but fog and tears. Bianca floated from the chair to the door, as if she had heard him calling. He smiled, his eyes growing bright for a moment as he saw her approach. She wiped her cheek with her hand and crawled up into the bed with him. He wrapped his thin arms around her, pulling her close to him and whispering into her ear. She nodded, and he smiled, stroking her hair for a moment.

Daniel's children stood in the doorway. Jack held Emma close to him, his hand smoothing her hair as she cried quietly into his chest. Robbie leaned against the wall, his face now devoid of emotion. He stood there staring off into space, his breathing short and choppy. Dean stood off to the side and out of the way, but he put his hand on my shoulder. I reached up and grabbed it, drawing on his strength to get me through this. We all stood there, waiting.

Daniel's hands went still. His chest stopped moving. But Bianca never let him go.

CHAPTER 28

resent Day

THE REST of the day was a blur. All I felt was pain, the gray shadows of memory taunting me with Daniel's life. He had been my friend, my father, and my employer. Despite months of preparation, it had come too soon. His absence left a hole in my heart that could never be filled.

The doctor entered the room, checking Daniel's limp wrist for a pulse. Bianca clung to him, her eyes shut as she willed him to still be alive. The doctor carefully worked around her, performing the necessary checks before quietly leaving the room. He put his hand on Jack's shoulder as he left, murmuring the words, "I'm sorry," he said, and Jack nodded, but I don't think he actually heard him. His eyes were glued to the bedroom, tears silently running down his face.

Upon the doctor's apology, Robbie stood. He stared at those of us in the doorway for a moment before taking off down the stairs. I heard the front door slam, but I let him go. A minute later, I could hear the roar of an engine as he drove off. I hoped he was going to his boat. At least he could find solace there.

Time passed, but no one else moved. A light touch on my shoulder from one of the funeral home attendants told me they had arrived. We shifted awkwardly from the door; my legs were numb, as though they had fallen asleep. I wondered what time it was, but realized that I didn't care.

The attendants went to Daniel's body, but Bianca refused to leave her beloved husband. He was gone, but she held onto him and refused to let go. Jack, Emma, and I had to pull her off of him. Her screams and pleas rang in my ears as we slowly coaxed her off the bed. As Daniel was taken away, she collapsed to the floor, sobs racking her body as Jack took her in his arms. He held her, the two of them rocking slowly back and forth as he let her cry.

I turned and left, not wanting to see her pain. My own chest felt like lead. It was hard to move, and I just wanted to curl up in a ball and hide. Or wake up and find out it'd it all just been a horrible dream. I wished Dean could take me up in his arms, to just let him hold me and take my pain away. But we couldn't.

He found small ways to make it easier, though-- pushing food in front of me, telling me I needed to eat as I attended to business. He would put his hand on my shoulder whenever he walked by, and he gave me a kiss on the cheek when he thought no one else was around. We had to be careful not to appear as anything more than friends.

I finally locked myself in the guest room to work. I had to notify the shareholders, the media, and the company, as well as put the funeral plans into motion. I went through my job like a robot, my head in a gray fog of loss, but getting things done nonetheless. I tried not to think about anything.

I woke up the next morning, still fully clothed on the guest bed, my hair messy and my face smeared with tears. I didn't even remember falling asleep. I zombie-walked to the shower, turning on the water so it would warm up. I stood there staring at the rising steam and I wished I could have Dean with me. I gave serious thought to texting him, so that he might come to my room and hold me in the shower.

Before I knew what I was doing-- before I even bothered to think of the consequences-- my phone was open, and I was calling Dean's number. He picked up on the second ring.

"Can you get away for a little bit? I'd like to see you," I said. I felt breathless and giddy.

"I'll be there in just a minute," Dean answered. The phone went silent, and I stared at it in my hand. *What am I doing?* I thought to myself. If we got caught, both our jobs would be up for evaluation from the board. Jack and Emma wouldn't have any say in it because we broke the rules of the employee contract. But I needed him.

There was a soft knock on the door, and I hurried to unlock it. Dean stood in the hallway, his eyes almost gray with worry.

"Are you okay? I came by last night but the door was locked, and you weren't answering." He stepped into the room, closing the door behind him. "I was worried about you."

As soon as the door was shut, I fell into him. He wrapped his arms around me, holding me close to him. My worry and pain seemed to fade as long as he was touching me. When he was with me, I felt like things were going to be all right. It didn't hurt so much when he could help carry my heavy heart.

"I'm sorry. I just crashed." My words were muffled by his chest. He took a deep breath and smoothed my hair.

"It's okay," he said, and kissed the top of my head. "Is your shower running?"

I pulled back with a sheepish grin. He cocked his head a little, clearly wondering what I was up to.

"I was actually hoping you might join me." I bit my lip. There were hundreds of reasons he should say no, but I hoped he would say yes. He hesitated for a moment, then smiled.

"Get in the water," he said, giving me a gentle push toward the bathroom. I wasn't sure he was coming until he started untying his shoes. "You've got fifteen minutes before I have to be anywhere."

I gave him the biggest smile I could manage and hurried to the bathroom door. He padded behind me on bare feet, stripping his shirt as he went. Inside the bathroom, I pulled yesterday's dirty shirt over my head, shaking my hair free of what was left of my bun.

Steam was filling the tiled bathroom, but I could still clearly see the definition in Dean's chest. I shimmied out of my pants, and quickly slipped off my undergarments before stepping into the hot water. It felt marvelous to get clean.

The glass door clicked shut as Dean walked in behind me.

The water came down hard and hot, pounding on my head and soaking me from head to toe. It felt wonderful. My shoulders eased down as the stress, sweat, and tears from the night before washed away. I closed my eyes, losing myself to the steady thrum of the water on my head. I could feel Dean behind me, a solid presence that was waiting patiently for me with a bottle of shampoo in his hands.

I stepped out of the flow of water, slowly wiping my eyes and looking up at Dean. He carefully poured shampoo into his hand, clicked the top shut, and moved in next to me. The water bounced off my skin and onto his, his tattoo starting to shine in the water. With gentle hands, he worked the suds into my hair. His fingers made slow circles, massaging my scalp. I closed my eyes, focusing only on the wonderful sensation of being cared for.

He braced one hand against my forehead, pushing me back gently into the shower head. The hot water sluiced through my hair, but because of his hand, never went near my eyes. The shampoo suds slid down my back as he gently worked the soap out of my hair.

When my hair was fully rinsed, he released his hand and reached for the bottle of conditioner, letting me stay in the water as he poured it into his hand. I stepped out, blinking water droplets from my eyelashes as he again worked his hands through my hair. He combed my wet tresses with his fingers, never pulling as he worked the conditioner into every strand of dark hair. It was the most luxurious, and intimate, experience of my life. He leaned me back into the water again, working the conditioner out of my hair in the hot water. I loved Dean for taking care of me when I needed it most.

From out of nowhere, a sob escaped my chest. I hadn't even realized I had been holding it in, but once released, the dam broke. Dean pulled me into him. His strong arms held me in place, and his body was a rock I could cling to as I drowned in my grief.

I lost my place in time. Everything hurt as the world

crumbled away until the only thing left was Dean. He didn't let me go. My tears mingled with the water, splashing across his chest and then down the drain. He held me until the tears stopped.

When I pulled back and my sobs had been reduced to sniffles, he kissed my forehead and gave me one of his special smiles. I rinsed my reddened face in the hot water. I felt drained, but stronger now. I heard the shower click as Dean stepped out. I stayed in the water for a moment longer, letting it wash away the last of my tears before I turned it off.

Dean was waiting for me, a towel wrapped around his slender waist. He had a large cream-colored towel held open and waiting to envelop me. I nearly started crying again because of his thoughtfulness. He wrapped me in the warm towel, slowly patting me dry. He worked his way from my shoulders, down my back, across my stomach, and down my legs. His hands were strong yet gentle as he blotted the moisture with the soft towel.

When he finished, he rose from my feet to kiss the tip of my nose. I gave him a soft smile, and he opened the door to the bedroom. Our clothes lay strewn across the floor. He quickly slid back into his dark pants and jacket, assuming the professional demeanor of a bodyguard. He watched with twinkling eyes as I pulled a dress from the closet and slid it over my body. I couldn't help but feel a warm glow when he looked at me.

As I ran a brush through my hair, he glanced at his watch and grimaced. I had completely lost track of time and had a horrible suspicion that we had gone over his fifteen minute window.

I considered leaving my hair down, the wet strands brushing gracefully against the dark fabric of the conservative dress, but I pulled it up into my traditional bun. I quickly finished in the bathroom and tucked the dirty clothes into the closet to throw in the wash later.

I opened my door, peeking out from side to side to make sure no one was coming. We didn't want to risk both of us coming out of my room with wet hair. I was about to tell him it was all clear when Emma walked by. She gave me a curious look, stopping for a moment.

"You okay? You look nervous," she said. I could tell she had been crying, but she was putting on a brave face. "The lawyer is running a little late, but the plan is still to have the reading in the parlor."

I nodded. Daniel had asked for his will to be read the day after his death. He had everything in order and had hoped it would help his family, and company, move on quicker.

"Thanks, Emma. I'll go make sure Bianca's ready," I said, hoping she would continue on down the hall. Dean hid behind the door. I could feel him twitching to get out, running late himself.

Emma nodded and finally progressed down the hall. She slouched as she walked, moving slowly. It seemed like an eternity before she was finally far enough out of sight that Dean could escape.

"I'll see you later, okay?" he whispered, kissing my cheek softly before ducking out the door. I watched him hurry down the hall and toward the guard station to check the incoming visitors into the house, his hair still glistening with water. I then carefully closed the door and headed to Bianca's room.

I stepped into her room, expecting to find her still in bed. Instead, she was dressed, making the bed herself. Her movements were quick and almost frantic, as though she were desperately trying to distract herself.

"Bianca?" I stepped closer to her, smelling her sweet perfume. It was Daniel's favorite, the one she only wore for special occasions.

"He always made the bed. Before the maids could do it, he would make it. Even in hotels." Bianca stared at the bedspread. "I hate making beds, but it didn't feel right to leave it that way."

I wrapped my arms around her, the hairspray in her hair crunching against my jaw. Her whole body was shaking, but she kept her face perfectly still. I took her hand, guiding her downstairs to the kitchen. I had a feeling she wasn't going to eat, but I needed to at least put the food in front of her. She sat staring out the window the rest of the morning, letting the coffee and eggs cool without ever touching them. When it came time for the reading of the will, she followed me like I was guiding her on a leash.

CHAPTER 29

 *resent Day*

THE SAUNDERS CLAN sat quietly in the parlor. Emma and Jack were on an old-fashioned love seat, Emma's head resting on Jack's shoulder. Robbie stood beside them, staring out the window, his hands behind his back. Several employees and close staff huddled in a group by the corner, solemn and quiet like a silent flock of black birds. I stood next to Bianca, who sat stiffly in a blue wing-backed chair. Her hair was perfect, her makeup unsmudged, but I knew inside she was screaming with loss.

A lawyer fumbled with long sheets of paper at the head of the room, preparing to read the will. Daniel had only been dead for less than a day, but it was per his wishes that the will be read now. I swallowed my tears down. Now that I was here, Daniel's death was real again. For a few blessed moments with Dean, my heart forgot to hurt. Now it just ached as though it were making up for the missed time.

Bianca's brown eyes stared blankly at the room. I knew she didn't see the people there, the flowers starting to arrive by the armload. She was lost in her own world.

The lawyer cleared his throat and began the proceedings. Everyone faced forward, their eyes looking at the lawyer, but I don't think very many of us were actually listening. Daniel had made his wishes known before his death, so I wasn't paying very much attention. The lawyer rattled on about the estate, the trusts, and so on. It was all what I had expected.

"... in addition to the aforementioned shares, a seat on the board of directors shall be given to Rachel Weber. She will no longer be an employee of DS Oil and Gas, but rather a partial owner of the company," the lawyer read. My eyes suddenly focused on him, but the lawyer was already reading the next section.

Bianca squeezed my arm, giving me a soft smile. "He told me he was going to do that. He always considered you a part of our family, and now, you have a part of the company, like you should, since you're our daughter."

I stared blankly at her, desperately trying to wrap my head around what Daniel had just done. A moment ago I was just a thousandaire, but now I was a billionaire.

THE LEAVES FLUTTERED OUTSIDE, their oranges and browns floating to the ground and turning the grass to gold. The sky was a brilliant blue with soft wisps of clouds riding the highest winds. The breeze shook the branches of the tree outside, but beside the window in Daniel's study, it was warm and safe. I sat in Daniel's big leather chair, my feet curled up under me as I stared across his empty desk. It felt like he was still here. The books and the globe were still the same. In this room, I could imagine he wasn't gone and I could ask him what he had meant by giving me a part of his company.

"Hey, partner," Jack said, poking his head in the door. "I thought I might find you here."

I stayed quiet as Jack entered, shutting the door behind him and moving to the window. Outside was the field where the boys and their father had played football on fall afternoons like this one. He pulled a book from the wall, thumbing through it and looking at me.

"I have no idea what just happened." I slumped in my seat.

"Dad gave you a part of the company and put you on the board of directors. Even I got that," he said, flicking the book shut. He gave me a devilish smirk.

I rolled my eyes at him. "No, I got that part. But what does that even mean? What kind of responsibilities does that entail? What's going to happen? Why did he do that?"

Jack sat on the edge of the desk. "Well, it means that you have a ridiculous amount of money. I could stop paying you, and you would never even notice. As far as responsibilities, Robbie is on the board. That should tell you all you need to know there. What happens next is up to you. You can keep your current job, which I would appreciate, or you can quit and retire to Tahiti." He stopped looking up at the sky as he continued. "Finally, he did it because he loved you."

I put my feet on the floor and splayed my hands across the desk. Jack watched quietly as I worked it out in my head. "This room reminds me of him. You remind me of him a lot, actually." I half-smiled as I pointed to a corner. "You used to do your homework at a little desk over there while he worked."

Jack's lips twitched up and the corners of his eyes crinkled. "I remember. I would pretend I was running the company, just like him."

In my mind, I could see Jack as a little boy, proudly displaying his finished assignment to a young Daniel. Daniel would always smile with satisfaction and tell him how proud he was of him.

"He knew about you and Dean," Jack said softly.

"I know. I told him when Dean was hired that we had been together." I fidgeted with my hands. With all the turmoil, I hadn't asked Jack about the employee contracts yet.

Jack shifted his perch on the desk for a more direct look at me. "No, I mean that the two of you are meant to be together. My Dad thought of you as his little girl, the princess that no man would ever be worthy of. That's why he was so adamant about you following the employee dating policy. He didn't think Dean was good enough for you."

My hands stilled, and I frowned up at Jack. "What made him change his mind?"

Jack smiled, his hazel eyes twinkling in the sunshine. "Emma. Or rather how happy Emma makes me. He could see the chemistry between the two of you. Though, honestly, a blind man could see that the two of you were trying not to see one another." Jack put his hand on my shoulder and continued in a soft voice. "He finally saw that Dean was your Prince Charming. He wanted you to be happy, so he just gave you the coach and glass slippers. Dad did even better than a fairy godfather, though. It won't disappear at midnight."

I opened my mouth, but no sound came out. I didn't have words. Jack patted my hand gently before he slid off the edge of the desk. He stood next to the window, staring out at the changing leaves. He looked so much like his father.

The room was quiet and the wind hummed a strange tune through the trees. I felt lost. Daniel had just given me the best gift of my life, but I was suddenly afraid. I was afraid that after all this time, it wouldn't work out. Afraid that our passion was really just an illusion that would fade once it was allowed to face the sun.

I closed my eyes, and imagined Dean's face. How his eyes could be ice blue and yet fill me with warmth; the curve of his lips when he smiled that cocky half-smile that sent my heart into spasms. I remembered how amazing it had felt to wake up in the middle of the night and find him sleeping next to me. I remembered that kiss in the car and how my heart soared knowing he still cared.

We still had our issues. Twenty years of thinking someone forgot about you wouldn't be easy to forget, but I wanted to. I didn't want to live the next twenty years knowing that I had missed out on something amazing, hiding behind an employee contract, because I was too chicken to actually give love a chance. I loved Dean. I had since the moment I met him, and I never stopped, even when all common sense told me I should have.

I looked up at Jack. My mind was made up. I was going to be with Dean. I loved him and I wasn't going to let my own fears and expectations stop us from being happy.

"So, if I keep my current job, does that mean I get a raise?" I asked Jack. He rolled his eyes at me.

"No. In fact, I think I might cut your hours a bit. Emma keeps telling me you have promised to design a dress for her, and so far you have been too busy to do it." Jack held his hand up to the side of his mouth as though he were letting me in on a secret. "I like to keep her happy, so you're going to need to do it soon."

"I guess my rent is still going to be paid by DS Oil and Gas one way or another," I said, a smile creeping onto my face.

"Well, with your new status upgrade, you now qualify to get an assistant. Choose wisely, because they will run your life." Jack gave me a wink.

"Yeah, I don't know. I'm never going to get one as good as me anyway," I said with a shrug. Jack reached across the desk and punched my arm.

"You'll find one. Just look for someone who's good at math. Or at least math tricks," Jack said. I stood up and I embraced him. He pulled me in close to him, hugging me tight.

"Hey, a girl's gotta breathe," I gasped as he squeezed as tight as he could. Jack let me go, keeping a hand on my shoulder.

"Dean's downstairs in the garden. If you need anything, let me know. I'm going to stay up here for a little bit," Jack said, glancing around the room. His shoulders dropped, and his eyes went distant as he looked around his father's office.

"Thank you, Jack. Thank you for everything." I gave him another quick hug.

"Get down there and tell that man that you love him and can't stand to spend another minute apart. Please. The rest of us are going to get sick off your lovey eyes if you don't." Jack shooed me with his hands toward the door. I looked back just before I closed it to see Jack sit in his father's chair. It might have been just a trick of the light, the way the dust motes fell through the sunshine, but I swear, for a moment, it looked as though Daniel was standing behind him with his hands on his son's shoulders, and smiling.

CHAPTER 30

 resent Day

THE AFTERNOON SUN transformed the world into a kaleido-
scope of orange and red as it filtered through the autumn
leaves. Dean sat in the garden on a wrought iron bench, his
eyes closed as he looked toward the sun. He reminded me of
a cat, sitting there soaking up the last rays of warmth before
winter.

I stood for a moment under the rustling leaves, just
admiring him. He was so handsome. His dark hair ruffled in
the fall breeze, the wind mussing it like a lover's caress. His
jaw was strong and smooth, his back tall and straight. Even
after all this time, he still made my heart pound in my chest
like a nervous school girl's. He was everything I could ever
ask for; everything I could ever want.

The leaves crackled under my feet as I followed the
stone pathway to the bench. Dean opened one eye just
enough for a sliver of blue to peek out, but then he closed it.

His face remained impassive. I smiled at him, even though he couldn't see it. I felt like I might vibrate out of my boots. I wanted to run to him, throw my arms around his neck and tell him we could be together, but instead, I behaved like an adult and sat down next to him.

I could see why he picked this spot. It was sheltered from the cold autumn wind and perfectly positioned to catch the afternoon sun. The garden was empty, as everyone else was inside and out of the fall weather. It was quiet, peaceful, and we were wonderfully alone. The iron was warm on my back, but the air crisp and clean. It was a beautiful afternoon. Daniel would have enjoyed it.

"Did you hear the will?" I asked, breaking the silence. Dean tensed slightly beside me, but he didn't move.

"Yeah. You're a billionaire now. Congratulations. I'm sure you're very happy." His voice was flat and dispassionate. It was almost as though he were angry, but I couldn't figure out why. We were going to be together.

"You know I'd rather have Daniel alive than the money," I said, feeling a frown tighten across my face. A cloud passed in front of the sun, blocking its warmth. Without it shining down, I was very aware of the oncoming winter chill.

Dean sighed and turned to me. "I know. I know how much he meant to you. How much they all mean to you. Daniel, Emma, Jack, even Bianca-- they're your family. They're your world."

I didn't know what to say to that, but he wasn't done speaking. He frowned, the corners of his perfect mouth going thin. "I have a job offer in LA. A rising starlet. I leave next week."

The ground seemed to crumbled beneath me like an autumn leaf. I shook my head as if hit by his words. "Please don't take it." The words came out as a whisper as if the wind had been knocked out me.

Dean took my hands in his, their warmth in stark contrast to the cold I was feeling. His blue eyes were earnest, and I could see the emotion rolling through them like storm clouds. "I can't take being here, being this close to you and not being able to touch you. To sit in a room with you and not be able to hold your hand. I want to kiss you all the time. I want to be able to comfort you, but I know that if I do, we'll lose everything we've worked for. I can't do that to you. You love these people too much for me to ask you to give them up."

"But we can be together now. Things have changed." I couldn't get the words out fast enough. He thought that he needed to leave me in order to keep me with the people I loved, but I could have them *and* him. We didn't have to choose between love and duty. Not again.

"What?" Dean's voice cracked slightly, his hands tightening around mine. Hope shone in his eyes, but he held it in check, as though afraid it could disappear. The sun came out from behind the cloud, bathing the two of us in golden light.

"Daniel made me an executive of the company. Not an employee. Executives can date employees. How do you think Jack was able to take his secretary to the Caribbean? As an executive, I can do whatever I want." My voice trembled as I gently touched his cheek. "And what I want, is you."

The smile that lit up Dean's face was the sweetest one I had ever seen. He reached for me, wrapping his arms around me and finding my mouth with his. My world dissolved into golden euphoria. The sun shone down, the leaves fluttered, and the grass slept. We were happy.

Dean kissed my forehead, his smile brightening my

world better than any sun. His lips brushed my skin as he whispered, "You're all I've ever wanted."

Pure joy bubbled up in my core, making my fingers tingle and my eyes start to water with uncontainable bliss. The man of my dreams, the one I had always wanted, the one that had always wanted me, was finally mine. There were no boundaries. We could have love and duty, without sacrificing either. I smiled as I kissed him, knowing that we had a beautiful future together.

EPILOGUE

*E*mma smiles at me. She fixes my veil one last time, making sure it is still on straight, then smooths the hair curling gently around my shoulders. She says something about weddings, and I smile automatically. My mind isn't on her. It's on the person waiting for me at the end of the stone pathway. Dean is waiting for me.

She fusses with Jack's tie, making sure that it, too, is on straight. He gives her a warm smile and shoos her out of the house. I can hear her heels clicking on the steps as she hurries to the garden to tell them we're ready to begin. I feel like I'm going to float away I'm so happy. I wonder how it is possible for any one person to brim with so much joy to the point of overflowing, yet here I am, barely able to contain myself.

Dean is waiting for me.

Jack takes my hand, placing it in the crook of his arm as we start to walk out the main doors. I remember my flowers at the last moment and I pull myself free to grab them. I grasp them tightly as I give my hand back to Jack. He smiles at my excitement and gives my arm a squeeze.

Dean is waiting for me.

The sun makes me blink as we step out of the Saunders'
mansion, but my eyes quickly adjust. Jack helps me navigate the
stairs with my heels and floor-length dress. I love my dress. It's
simple but elegant. I feel beautiful, and Dean is going to love it.
I'm so excited I have to refrain from running to the garden I'm so
excited.

Dean is waiting for me.

As soon as we enter, music begins to play. I don't really
hear it.

Dean is waiting for me.

He's standing in the gazebo, his blue eyes bright, wearing that
crooked grin I love. I can feel the smile on my face somehow grow
wider. My feet glide just above the stones as Jack escorts me to the
man I love.

Dean is waiting for me.

Jack shakes Dean's hand and gives me a hug. I can feel tears
in my eyes as he lets me go. Jack gives me beaming grin and
returns to his wife. There are only a few people sitting in the
garden, but that's how Dean and I wanted it. I can see Jenny and
Kimberly sitting with Sheriff Grinswald. Bianca wipes a tear
from her cheek.

Dean's hands are warm as he takes mine in his. I wonder if
he can feel me shaking. It's not because I'm nervous; it's because
I'm excited. I get to have the love of my life. After today, we won't
ever have to be apart again. My heart soars at the thought.

The minister asks me a question, and I answer it with a
simple, "I do." Dean repeats the words. I don't need to hear the
minster ask the words because I've already promised them in
my heart.

Dean slides a ring onto my finger. A diamond catches the sun,
sparkling with a thousand rainbows. My heart speeds up, threat-
ening to dance out of my chest. I've never felt this happy before,
this complete. I slip a thick silver band onto his hand, the two of

us now linked. Our rings bind us so we will never be apart again. All I can see is Dean's smile.

Dean raises the veil, carefully revealing my face. His own is beaming with joy. All I want is to kiss him, and as he leans forward, my wish is granted. Our lips touch, and he pulls me in to him. The sunlight sparkles through the trees, and I close my eyes, taking everything in. This moment is ours, just mine and Dean's, forever.

I barely notice the walk back into the house. I'm so happy holding onto Dean's strong arm that I barely notice the steps. Inside, the house is cool and quiet, just the two of us. I giggle, and Dean kisses me again, his lips sweet and wonderful as they merge with mine. I could kiss him every second of every day and love every minute of it.

He gives me one of his mischievous grins, pulling me to a small table. A bottle of champagne and two glasses sit, ready to be drunk. He hands me one, taking the other in his fingers. With a gentle clink, he taps them together and whispers, "To making new marriages."

The champagne bubbles in my mouth, tickling my nose and making me smile. I want to kiss him again, and because we are now married, I can.

I kiss him, tasting the effervescent champagne still on his lips. We share our champagne kisses, knowing we will have many more. I kiss him, feeling my heart soar in my chest, remembering our first champagne kiss. It took twenty years, but Dean and I are finally together. Everything is perfect.

WHAT IF TONY HADN'T DIED?

No doubt Kim would have been happier in life. I thought the same thing, so I felt compelled to write a novella describing Kim going back in time, to find Dean's battle buddy Tony and save him from dying in Operation Desert Storm. I hope you enjoy this novella I wrote as part of the "Fountain of Love"!

~

How do you convince the man you love to believe the impossible?

Poor Kimberly has spent her entire life pining for a man that will never return her affections. After spending a fantastic week in the summer of 1990 together, handsome and charming Tony Frontera made a promise that he would return to Kim after Operation Desert Storm. Unfortunately, he broke that promise when he was killed in action.

Kim spent the next two decades trying to fill the hole that he left in her life, but it never happened. Despite a rewarding career, she never found true happiness, the happiness that she should have had with Tony...

When the Fountain of Love suddenly grants her deepest wish, she finds herself back in 1990 in her old body, able to change the hand that fate dealt her. However, the power of the fountain is limited- in order to change Tony's fate, she must do the impossible. Although she had dreamt about saving Tony, she never thought about *how* she would do it. With only your words, how do you convince your soul mate that you are from the future? How do you tell them to abandon their country and leave everyone they know behind?

If you enjoyed *Champagne Kisses*, you will love this side story to Rachel and Dean's timeless love story.

Found exclusively on Krista's website.

THANK YOU FOR READING!

Thank for you reading until the end. My husband served for nine years in the United States Army, and Champagne Kisses has always been my favorite. I hope that you'll check out some of my other books.

Don't forget to join my mailing list as well for updates! (clickable link)

IF YOU LIKED THIS BOOK…

Escape With Me: A Midlife Love Story

"I gave it all up to be happy. I'd give it all up again for you."

They say life begins after 40, but Cassie ain't feelin' it. Divorced and feeling trapped by her job, she wants to let loose for her friend's tropical beach wedding. She decides to let her hair down and get a little unpredictable. That's when she meets a handsome bartender, Wyatt.

Despite a few grey hairs, Wyatt's the liveliest man that Cassie has ever met. She knows that there's got to be more to his life story than just being a bartender, but this is just supposed to be a vacation fling. And after sunny days spent breaking all the rules on the beach together, Cassie realizes that nobody has ever listened to her the way that Wyatt does.

His carefree life is enviable, his kisses are intoxicating, and she can almost imagine a life with him. But all vacations come to an end. And when Cassie invites him to visit her hometown, Wyatt reveals that he can never go back. Not to her town. Not to America. Not to civilization.

Cassie leaves, confused and heartbroken, wondering just who she got herself involved with. Suddenly, her predictable life gets turned upside down when she sees her picture splashed across the Internet. And when the tabloids come looking for the mature woman who found the lost billionaire, she has no idea what to do...

...until he comes back.

Escape With Me: A Midlife Love Story

ABOUT THE AUTHOR

New York Times and USA Today Bestseller Krista Lakes is a thirtysomething who recently rediscovered her passion for writing. She is living happily ever after with her Prince Charming. Her first kid just started preschool and she is happy to welcome her second child into her life, continuing her "Happily Ever After"!

Thank you for supporting an indie author. Anything you can do, whether it be writing a review, or even simply telling a fellow reader that you enjoyed this, helps me out immensely. Thanks!

Krista would love to hear from you! Please contact her at Krista.Lakes@gmail.com or friend her on Facebook!

Further reading:

Bad Boys and Babies
  Family Doctor's Baby
  The Billionaire's Baby Arrangement
  Crime Boss Baby

Kinds of Love
  A Forever Kind of Love
  A Wonderful Kind of Love
  An Endless Kind of Love

Billionaires and Brides

Yours Completely: A Cinderella Love Story

Yours Truly: A Cinderella Love Story

Yours Royally: A Cinderella Love Story

The "Kisses" series

Saltwater Kisses: A Billionaire Love Story

Kisses From Jack: The Other Side of Saltwater Kisses

Rainwater Kisses: A Billionaire Love Story

Champagne Kisses: A Timeless Love Story

Freshwater Kisses: A Billionaire Love Story

Sandcastle Kisses: A Billionaire Love Story

Hurricane Kisses: A Billionaire Love Story

Barefoot Kisses: A Billionaire Love Story

Sunrise Kisses: A Billionaire Love Story

Waterfall Kisses: A Billionaire Love Story

Island Kisses: A Billionaire Love Story

Other Novels

I Choose You: A Secret Billionaire Romance

His Every Desire: A Billionaire Seduction

Wolf Six's Salvation: A Shifter Love Story

Burned: A New Adult Love Story

Walking on Sunshine: A Sweet Summer Romance

An American Cinderella: A Royal Love Story

Mr. Darcy's Kiss: A Contemporary Pride and Prejudice